Brocade Valley

Wang Anyi

Brocade Valley

Translated by Bonnie S. McDougall & Chen Maiping

NEW DIRECTIONS

Manufactured in the United States of America
New Directions Books are printed on acid-free paper
First published clothbound by New Directions in 1992
Published simultaneously in Canada by Penguin Books Canada Limited

Library of Congress Cataloging-in-Publication Data
Wang, An-i.
    [Chin-hsiu ku chih lien. English]
    Brocade Valley / Wang Anyi ; translated by Bonnie S. McDougall & Chen Maiping.
      p. cm.
    ISBN 0-8112-1224-6 (alk. paper)
    I. Chen, Maiping. II. McDougall, Bonnie S. III. Title.
PL2919.A584713 1992
895.1'352—dc20   92-18529
                                                  CIP

New Directions Books are published for James Laughlin by
New Directions Publishing Corporation,
80 Eighth Avenue, New York 10011

INTRODUCTION

THE AUTHOR

At the beginning of the 1980s, Wang Anyi enjoyed a reputation as a promising young author. Her mother, Ru Zhijuan, was a well-known writer whose stories in the 1950s and 1960s were orthodox products typical of intellectuals who supported the Communist regime. She was also one of the first of the established writers of her generation to suggest through her fiction in the early 1980s that intellectuals might take a more independent stance in society. Wang Anyi started her career as a writer on a similar note, and her mildly innovative, subtly critical fiction was greeted approvingly by official literary circles with national awards in 1983 and 1985. In these years, Chinese intellectuals were encouraged to express their views with unprecedented openness—even the underground writers of the Cultural Revolution had access to the national press. Wang Anyi then took a bold step: choosing extramarital sex as her focus, she suddenly emerged as a trend-setter rather than a follower, somewhat to the consternation of the authorities who had treated her so benignly.

The three novellas that brought public fame to Wang Anyi in 1986–1987 were all on the theme of women exploring socially unacceptable relationships in an officially puritanical society. The first two stories set sexual obsession within conventionally moralistic frames: in the third novella, translated here, the sexually adventurous woman is not punished for her activities but on the contrary, is awarded a highly modernistic prize—a new sense of self which enables her to author her own story.

THE STORY

The trilogy begins with *Romance on a Barren Mountain,*[1] a tale of two couples linked by an affair between one wife and the other husband, ending in the suicide of the adulterous husband at his lover's instigation. *Romance in a Small Town,*[2] the second, describes two young provincial dancers seized by an overwhelming passion which destroys the man but provides eventual salvation for the woman in the birth and rearing of their child. *Romance in Brocade Valley* (translated here as *Brocade Valley*) is the third and most controversial: the story of a young married woman who establishes her own identity through a brief affair. In all three, the heroine is the dominant partner in the relationship as well as the center of the story.

Wang Anyi is not a feminist in the sense now understood in the West. In a recently published comment on women and women's writing, she denies that social and economic discrimination against women exists in China, advocates restricted employment for women below a certain educational level, and associates women's writing with negative characteristics such as weakness, self-indulgence and over-ornamentation. Given the striking differentials in job opportunities and wages for women in contemporary China, such statements by Wang Anyi should be read as a form of internalized self-censorship in a highly controlled context. The fact that her interlocutor on this occasion was a woman writer from Taiwan makes the issue even more sensitive.

Additionally, as is true of most writers in China, Wang Anyi suffers from a system whereby writers are paid by the word (over and above state salaries for the established authors). The heroine's tactful approach to her work as a manuscript editor in *Brocade Valley* gives a misleading impression of publishing in China, where editorial intervention is so crudely politicized that no effectual constraint is offered (or accepted) on literary grounds. The playfulness of Wang Anyi's device in creating a triple persona for the heroine—as narrator, protagonist, and projection—is evidence of the latitude given to literary style in the mid-80s, but readers might have been grateful if her editors had exerted more control over the repetition that Wang Anyi relies on as a unifying or atmospheric device (somewhat modified in this translation).

Nevertheless, Wang Anyi must be seen as a major figure among official Chinese writers of the 1980s. The sexual puritanism and patriarchal images of women which have characterized official Chinese writing for decades are undermined in ground-breaking ways in her work. The sexual passion between the poorly educated lovers in *Small Town* is depicted, conventionally enough, as brutish lust for which both must pay a price, and yet the description of the couple's awakening sensuality is the most detailed and complex in contemporary fiction. On a different level altogether, sexual flirtation by a bored working wife from a much higher educational background is, in a profoundly subversive manner, elevated in *Brocade Valley* into a self-justifying quest for selfhood beyond any consideration of personal ethics or social morality.

Discrimination between women from different social classes and educational backgrounds, with education as the factor which frees *Brocade Valley*'s protagonist from moral judgment, is equally far from socialist realism and modern feminism. Wang Anyi, despite the prudence of non-fictional comments in her interview, allows her perceptions to drive her fictional creations with great power and sensibility. Her dedication to the ideals of individualism and self-respect produce female portraits of a depth and complexity rarely found in Chinese literature of any era. Western readers might find the heroine overly glamorized; this is not a problem for most Chinese readers who expect the author to identify with characters of this kind. Authorial distance as practiced by Wang Anyi in *Small Town* would have been seen as a betrayal of intellectuals—especially of women intellectuals in the literary world—had it been exercised in *Brocade Valley*.

THE SETTING

Western readers might find it hard to visualize the physical details of the setting. The following descriptions of the apartment, the office, the hotel, and the resthouse are based on those I've seen occupied or visited by Chinese acquaintances of roughly the same social standing as the protagonist.

The couple live in an urban apartment block, possibly

in the former French Concession in Shanghai, but dating from after the Communist takeover in 1949. The small entrance lobby is blocked with bicycles before and after work. There is no elevator, and the stairs would be poorly lit (if at all). The toilets and washrooms are communal, probably at the end of the corridor on each floor. The apartment itself consists of one big room to be used as a combination bedroom, living room, and dining room. Leading off it, either as an alcove or possibly just a curtained-off area, is a small kitchen with a gas stove and a sink with only cold running water. The stove probably has only two burners (no oven or broiler), and is connected to bottled gas. The overhead ceiling light in the main room is a relatively modern fixture and is therefore valued; lamps and candles would be a sign of backwardness or poverty.

The publishing house where the protagonist works is no great distance away, since she walks rather than rides her bicycle. It is an old Western-style building dating from Shanghai's days as an international trading city. Her office is a big room with several desks in it (very few people would have their own private office). Every morning when they come in, the editors wipe their desks and chairs, which get very dusty overnight because of the high level of air pollution. One of them also sweeps out the office. Twice a day, winter and summer alike, they fetch thermoses of hot water from boilers in the basement. Some people drink plain boiled water, some make tea from tea-leaves brewed in the cup (it is quite common to use a screw-top glass jar). Most Chinese people prefer a hot meal at lunchtime: there is a cafeteria in the basement, heavily subsidized but of poor quality. People bring their own enamel bowls and chopsticks or spoons, and rinse them in the washrooms after use.

Since it is an older building, the floor is wood (in their apartment it is probably concrete), and there is always an unpleasant noise when people get up or sit down, as the chair legs scrape against the bare boards. The day begins with the sound of an electric bell at 8 a.m., and finishes at 6 p.m. (or at one o'clock on Saturdays) with a final bell. At 10 a.m. and at 3 p.m. there are fifteen-minute exercise-breaks during which music is broadcast; some people practice *taiji* at this time, others duck out to do their daily shopping, read the newspaper, or simply talk. After lunch, many people like to stretch out on their desks and take naps. Work is conducted in a fairly leisurely fashion: there is time to read the newspapers, gossip, or daydream.

At the hotel and resthouse, it is normal for rooms to be shared by at least two people, and there is always a much larger number of men than women. Resthouses— or sanitoria—especially at popular resorts like Lushan, are usually no more than ordinary guest houses run by the state, and are often used for conferences. People of status (such as writers) on any official occasion (such as attending a conference) would always be met at the airport or train station by their host, usually a high-ranking official, and conveyed to and from their hotel by an official car. Smoking is still very common among men, less common among women.

Lushan (literally, Lu Mountain) is a famous scenic spot in central southern China, where Mao Zedong wrote a famous poem dedicated to his wife Jiang Qing. It was at a conference in Lushan in 1959 that Mao's policies were first challenged by other Party leaders; the conference would have been held in a resthouse much like the one in this story. In the more open and prosperous '80s, private tourism became popular in China, but for most office workers, travel on official business remained the most common form of tourism. The male writer is slightly blasé: it would not have been anything new for him. It may very well have been the heroine's first conference, however, and the glamour of the occasion is nicely matched by the magnificence of the setting.

THE TRANSLATION

The terms of address used in the heroine's office—Mr. Wang, Miss Zhang—are slightly more formal than in the original Chinese, which uses the common terms *lao* (literally "old": used roughly for colleagues who are male, older, senior, and/or physically bigger) and *xiao* (literally "small" or "young": used roughly for colleagues who are female, younger, junior, and/or physically smaller). On the other hand, they indicate something of the formality and tension commonly found in Chinese offices where colleagues are often obliged to inform on each other and rarely form close personal friendships.

Wang Anyi has developed a very fluid style, where sentences may run on for whole paragraphs, paragraphs occupy whole pages, and repetition of key phrases and passages is frequent. While its essential characteristics have been retained, the translation has been slightly modified for Western readers. The translators would like to express their thanks to the editor, Barbara Epler, for her very sympathetic and tactful editing of the text. We are also most grateful to Peggy L. Fox for her generous help and support in this project.

Bonnie S. McDougall
Edinburgh, June 1992

1. Translated as *Love on a Barren Mountain*, Renditions, Hong Kong, 1991.
2. Translated as *Love in a Small Town*, Renditions, Hong Kong, 1988.

Brocade Valley

The last typhoon of the year had come and gone, and the first leaves of autumn fell down sibilantly on the balcony. Night had sealed the glass-panelled door with darkness, but I could imagine a deep golden quilt out there. Later, it began to rain, large drops striking the fallen leaves with heavy plops. I didn't notice the rain ending, but after a while I no longer heard it. When I got up this morning, sunshine sparkled in every corner, but the fallen leaves were sodden and pasted, yellow-brown, over the balcony floor.

I want to tell a story, a story about a woman. The early autumn wind is fresh, the sunlight is clear and my mind is calm, and I can think about the story calmly. It occurs to me that this story also began after an autumn rain.

The autumn rain had come and gone. Sparkling sunshine lit up every corner, but the fallen leaves had rotted and lay, red-brown, pasted over the balcony floor. She got up and sat on the edge of the bed, drowsy and lethargic; her mouth was sour, a yawn rose in her throat, her eyes blurred with tears. Curling one leg over the side of the bed and letting the other hang down till her toes touched the floor, she gave her husband a sidelong look.

He lay on the bed, face up, arms and legs sprawled wide, occupying the half of the bed which she had just relinquished. The wind blew in the bamboo blind, shifting the morning sunlight; his body lay in darkness one minute and bathed in light the next. Her mind also shifted from dark to bright and back again, as if it were on a swing going up and down, until she felt slightly nauseous. But he still lay there without moving.

At last, as if he'd heard some kind of summons in his dream, he made an abrupt dogpaddling movement with his limbs, turned over, and sat up crosslegged on the bed. At first he sat there blankly, his eyes staring into nothingness as if in a trance. Absently he stretched out one hand and groped at the bedside cupboard. The first object his hand fell on was an earpick, and he proceeded to clean his ears. As the pick entered his ear, his eyes narrowed; a flicker of emotion passed across his face—finally some sign of life. However, he immediately sank into another stupor.

She sat there calmly, relaxed and at ease, watching him without seeming to. Then at last he was awake; the light of sense and reason dawned in his eyes. Seeing her seated on the edge of the bed, he asked about breakfast. She answered briefly, pointedly, and got to her feet. He let one leg down to the floor and crooked the other on the bed. The sun lit up the room through the bamboo blind.

She stood in the light and put her hair up in rollers. She used six rollers all together: two in front, two behind, and one on either side; they looked like a bizarre skullcap. He sat on the edge of the bed, silently counting the rollers on her head. She carried the gruel pot to the stove, then leisurely brushed her teeth and washed her face. He stood up and took a few steps forward just as she came back into the bedroom. Their shoulders touched as they passed. As he brushed his teeth at the sink, the sound of an electric hairdryer came from the bedroom.

When they joined each other at the kitchen table, both were immaculate. His gleaming white collar rubbed lightly against his jaw, still pale from shaving; he gave off the warm fresh fragrance of sandalwood soap as his hands drew bamboo chopsticks across the surface of the rice gruel in his bowl. Caught back behind her ears, the ends of her black hair curled towards her shining cheeks as naturally as if she had been born with wavy hair. Neither paid the slightest attention, however, as if they knew each other so intimately that there was no longer any possibility of mutual admiration.

Instead they concentrated on the gruel, eating hastily and not bothering how it tasted. Reheating the previous night's rice in boiling water makes a gruel hot enough to burn the mouth, and not easy to swallow. Very soon, their foreheads were beaded with sweat. She put down her chopsticks, stretched out, and turned on the electric fan, saying, "It's hot." "Yes, it's hot," he answered like an echo. When they finished the gruel it was precisely half-past seven, and he left. At twenty to eight she left as well.

Wearing a blue skirt and white blouse, she tripped down the grubby staircase like a young girl who still hasn't left home. The sunlight seemed transparent and a cool breeze flowed through the transparent sunlight. She lifted her face and let the wind blow her hair back, feeling her spirits rise.

It was a morning like every other morning—a morning like one of the better mornings. If anything were different about it, it was only that there were more muddy leaves than usual on the balcony, but she paid this no attention. She was so thoroughly familiar with her home that nothing about it could arouse her interest or curiosity. She was also well aware that there was no need for her to pay any attention to it. It was only when she went out the door that her life started. Being at home was no more than a preparation for life, like being back-stage before a performance.

Behind the locked double door, the fallen leaves on the balcony were gradually drying out. Peeling them-selves from the painted cement floor, they curled up, brushed softly against each other, and slipped away be-tween the railings.

She saw the withered leaves in the street, slipping between the trees along the pavement, the sunlight transforming them back into gold again. They tumbled and rolled in all their glory, brightening the whole street.

I must follow her, watching how she mischievously pursued the golden, curled-up leaves with her toe and playfully trampled them to hear them crackle, like a carefree university student—which was what the passers-by took her for, because of her slender figure which hadn't born a child, because of her neat simple clothes, because she carried a big bulky briefcase and not the usual small purse-size handbag. Some people couldn't help being jealous when they looked at her, jealous of the way she seemed so young and carefree. She herself was conscious of a sense of serenity. However, she was about to encounter something—yes, something was about to happen. I'm probably the only one on this street who knows it.

The street was a tranquil, tree-lined avenue of a kind rarely found in this city, and featured its most handsome buildings in traditional Chinese and Western styles. The French parasol-trees' branches thick with leaves intertwined above the street, forming a green corridor speckled with sunlight. Even if it had been very long she would have walked the whole way, never taking a bus. Unfortunately, it was very short. As soon as she turned out of it, losing the protection of the green shade, she became a little depressed and felt tired. However, the place where she worked—a white, four-story building that looked like a ship—was nearby, twinkling with strange lights (not white but azure), and her spirits revived. She even experienced a slight, habitual excitement. She was about to enter this building, a building where she had many colleagues both old and new. Whenever she was about to come into their presence, she would experience this excitement, almost every time without fail.

As she patted her hair, smoothing into place the curls that seemed so natural, she noticed that the sunlight which passed directly over the wall on the opposite side of the road threw her shadow on the near wall as on a mirror, and she couldn't help appreciating her own attractive figure.

Preoccupied, she had arrived at the top of the steps.

As the bell rang for starting work, people dashed up and down the stairs with their thermoses, momentarily too busy to greet her as they rushed to fetch hot water from the boiler room. Adding her footsteps to the confusion, she went up to the second floor and entered her own office.

The dregs of yesterday's tea were still there, and the glass desktop was covered with a thin layer of dust. Mr. Wang, whose desk faced hers, was sweeping the floor. When he reached her feet, she felt obliged to make an attempt to wrest the broom from him—naturally without success. She took her teacup to the lavatory to wash it, but the door was locked; someone was inside using it. As she was waiting, she glanced through a copy of yesterday's evening paper (which she'd already read) on someone's desk, and came across an item that was new to her.

The flush sounded and then the door opened. As she'd expected, Mr. Li emerged, a little embarrassed, his eyes averted. She brushed past him and went in. There was a smell of smoke inside, and in the white porcelain bowl a cigarette butt floated on the gradually rising water. She poured out the dregs, dipped a finger into some cleanser, and carefully washed out her teacup.

While she was doing this, someone else came in to empty her teacup and stood next to her washing it out. It was Miss Zhang, who had just gotten a new perm; her glossy black hair lay in waves over her shoulders. She praised her perm generously, after which Miss Zhang replied that hers was superior! Modestly she demurred, but inside her heart she had her own bright mirror. She listened patiently as Miss Zhang told her in detail how the hairdressing went and what she'd heard and who she'd seen at the salon, and when someone else came in to wash his hands, she took the opportunity to retreat.

The mail clerk had just been along and tossed several letters on her desk. She sorted through them briefly with her wet fingers (guessing for the most part who they were from and what they were about), and then went to make her tea. She'd just bought the first tea of the season, which she kept stored in a small teacaddy in the top left-hand drawer of her desk, together with a bowl and a pair of chopsticks in a muslin bag.

When the tea was ready, she sat down in her armchair. There were only ten armchairs altogether, which had been commandeered in order of seniority; newcomers were left with only narrow kitchen chairs to sit on. She was one of the first editors to be employed when the magazine was re-established after the Cultural Revolution, the youngest of the original founders. Over the next few years, a steady stream of university graduates were hired, each lot younger than the last, so that by now she was far from being the youngest. But it was her firm conviction that since she was the youngest editor when the magazine was revived, as long as that time remained the keystone of the structure defining her place in the universe, she would never grow old.

Leaning back in her chair, she gazed out the window. Outside stood a tall paulownia tree, transplanted from a remote area in northwest China. Through its dense leaves, she could see the small, red brick house in the neighboring courtyard, which had a pitched roof like a fairy-tale cottage and a semi-circular balcony.

I follow her gaze. Standing behind her, looking over her shoulder and out through the leaves of the paulownia tree, I can see a little girl run out of the small, red brick house. She pauses for a moment on top of the steps by the front door, then runs down, through the courtyard, and out the ornate black iron gate. Then a little old man comes into sight, hesitates, and slowly takes up a position outside the gate.

A trolleybus passes down the road. The conductor bangs the outside panel below the window, indicating that the bus is approaching the next stop.

She withdrew her gaze and languidly took up her mail. With a pair of scissors which were neither especially sharp nor dull, she slit open the envelopes one by one, pulled out the letters, and read them. A faint sense of expectation arose in her mind, but it was immeasurably distant and uncertain: she didn't know what she was expecting or why she should be expecting anything at all. When she finished her letters, her anticipations, not surprisingly, proved to have been in vain.

As if unwilling to let her expectations be altogether extinguished, the telephone rang. The telephone was close to her, and she stretched out her hand and picked up the receiver. It was not for her, however, but for Mr. Wang opposite. A woman was calling, possibly his wife, possibly not. He had already heard the voice on the other end of the line, had stopped what he was doing, and was waiting for her to pass him the receiver. Having handed it over, she had no further reason to sit there doing nothing: she must try to get something done.

She took the topmost manuscript from a small mountain lying on the cupboard behind her and placed it before her. The manuscripts were dull and mediocre, while the handwriting came in such a variety of grotesque and fantastic shapes and sizes that they were often impossible to read. Diligently she set to work.

Suddenly the noisy office fell silent, like the hitch that sometimes occurs when a film is being shown—the action continues but the sound is gone. The silence was a little uncanny, as if something were about to happen. But no one felt it was strange since they were all engrossed in their work, everyone thinking that the work they had in hand was of major importance, more important than anything else.

But the silence was only temporary. A bee flew in, creating a minor disturbance as it zoomed up, down, and around. Almost everyone stood up: some spread open their manuscripts to fan it away; others rolled up their books to wave it away; some suggested swatting it but others said that you shouldn't provoke it, that as long as you didn't provoke it nothing would happen but if you did you would certainly get stung. Not everyone believed this, yet nobody felt like being rash. The bee performed a final graceful dance and flew out the window, leaving golden rings in front of everyone's eyes which only slowly faded away. The babble of noise remained; the film continued with action and sound reunited.

Mr. Wang informed her that there would be a writers' conference at Lushan the following Monday, a small-scale affair but attended by the first and second rank of writers from all over the country; a large number of literary matters were to be discussed and it was expected to be very lively; their editorial office would probably send somebody to cover it.

She couldn't help letting her imagination run wild when she heard this: if only she could go, what would it be like? Her heart began to beat a little faster.

Mr. Li and Miss Zhang were engaged in gossip, their voices pitched very low, so low that only the whole room could hear. Without meaning to, she also listened in. Just at this moment, the music for the exercise break came over the loudspeaker. One by one her colleagues stood up, pushing their chairs back and then forward again on the waxed floor.

The sun was shining directly on the window next to her, and the glass flashed dazzlingly white. She moved away from the glaringly bright window towards one at the other end of the room facing a gloomy back lane. Water running down the drainpipe into the underground sewer made a gurgling sound. Sunlight couldn't penetrate into the lane, which was dark and desolate and bleak, but at the same time not without a certain warmth, as if one could hide there and be safe. Not a soul was in sight.

With her back to the radiant, golden window at the other end of the room, she gazed at the narrow dark lane, lost in thought. Indistinctly she heard someone calling her but she didn't answer, waiting for the second or third summons, or for no further summons at all. There were no further summons, and she remained alone, absorbed in her thoughts.

And so, facing the narrow lane, I remain thinking about my story.

There was nothing in the narrow lane, only potholes and a gurgling sewer. A gush of water tumbled down, filling the sewer, and rapidly disappeared underground; a few discordant notes and it was gone. The silence returned.

She was facing the narrow lane, her back to the gleaming window. The sun had moved slightly, so the light became a little milder and no longer dazzled the eye. At that moment, the exercise music concluded, and again the chairs glided back and forth on the floor as people one by one took their seats. She waited to see if somebody would call her but there was nothing, and finally she moved away and walked across the office towards her own place under the shining window.

Halfway across the room, or slightly more than halfway across the room—at this point there is a door to the right leading to a short corridor, and if you go up two steps and turn to the left, you come to the chief editor's office—she was just at this point close to the chief editor's office—

In her later days, in her future memories, this short passage, this crossing, would become very, very long, as long as half a lifetime—

Halfway across the room, just as she was about to pass the entrance to the chief editor's office, the deputy chief editor—there was no chief editor, the position was empty, there was only a deputy chief editor—came out of his room, paused at the top of the two steps, and said:

"The Lushan conference, it's yours!"

The deputy chief editor was standing at the end of a dark passageway. From behind him, through the half-opened door, a few rays of light outlined his figure.

Backlit in this way, he gave her a briefing on such things as the departure time and the meeting place, the reception personnel from the publishing house which was organizing the conference, and so on. Then he walked down the steps and bustled off, his briefcase in his hand, on his way to a hotel to meet a third-ranked writer who had come from far away; he'd been holding the briefcase while he was talking to her.

She completed the second half of her passage across the office back to her own desk. The sunlight shifted, it shone on another window, and then it shone on the window next to it, and then the lunch bell rang. Those who went home for lunch went home; those who didn't go home didn't. Not going home for lunch, she took her enamel bowl in its muslin bag and went downstairs to the cafeteria. The cafeteria was on the ground floor, next to the assembly hall, and was thick with steam from the vats of rice and smoke from the frying pans.

Twenty people were already standing in line, and the twenty people standing in line were talking to each other; she was the twenty-first and the twenty-first voice talking. She was talking but Lushan loomed in her head. She'd never been to the famous mountain resort; she'd never been to the mountains at all. The Lushan in her head was the cloud-wreathed Immortal's Cave celebrated in Mao's poem. She stood in front of the cave, wearing clothes that she'd made a long time ago but for a long time had had no chance to wear: a two-piece outfit, particularly suitable for Lushan's undoubtedly pleasant, cool summer weather. However, she couldn't see herself clearly—her clothes looked unfamiliar, as if they belonged to someone else, and she herself was equally unfamiliar. Still, she felt excited and spoke loudly, almost drowning out everyone else. When people looked at her, she became embarrassed. At that point it was her turn at the head of the line.

For the rest of the day she had plenty to occupy her mind, but she couldn't work quietly and found pretexts to chat with the others. From time to time she read a manuscript, even quite efficiently, but Lushan intruded, an indistinct presence in her mind—she had to think about Lushan while reading her manuscripts. Once, tired out by the effort of thinking of two things at the same time, she raised her head and looked out the window, determined to concentrate on one thought only, but she no longer knew what to think about, or even how to think. It was an effort to think of one thing at a time also. She lowered her head and turned back to her manuscripts. The mountain peak, wreathed in clouds and mist, moved behind the different styles of handwriting on the manuscripts.

She paid no further attention to the narrow lane on the far side, but the lane became inhabited. First there was a boy coming back home from school, who hammered on the back door and yelled till he became hoarse. Next came a man from out of town trying to exchange enamel pots and pans for ration tickets, who cried his wares entering and exiting like an opera singer. There was also sunlight in the lane, as the setting sun moved west, casting a yellow glow over the lane and reminding people of the night to come.

It gradually grew dark.

The day was nearing its end and she was weary. She looked wan, covered by a layer of invisible dust, and her clothes were crumpled, so wrinkled that they looked as if they'd been boiled. Her whole person presented a dismal sight. She longed to go home. Her desire to leave became intense. She felt unhappy and in her depression wanted to be home.

Her longing to go home had lasted for about an hour when finally the bell rang.

At dusk the avenue was mild and tranquil, but she rushed along, like every pedestrian at this time of day. No one was in the mood to pay attention to anyone else or attract any, but hurried on their way, on their journey home. Fortunately there was a gentle, refreshing breeze to comfort the depressed and weary bodies.

The sun had already set at the end of the street behind her, as if there were a city there where the sun made its home. Her back to the twilight, she hurried on and on, arriving home just as she reached the point of exhaustion. First she fished her keys out and opened the letter-box, but there was nothing in it except the evening paper; after a moment's reflection she realized that there wouldn't be anything more. She felt even wearier. Fatigue like a huge, shapeless animal bent over her swiftly, crushing her, and she needed her whole body to bear it, to support it.

Slowly she climbed upstairs. The handrail was completely rusted over and offered no support. The side wall, covered with obscene drawings, was piled high with rubbishy odds and ends; it was impossible even to get close to it. She was obliged to make her way upstairs unaided.

Some windows were lit up, others were still dark. In her own home, the window that looked onto the corridor was pitch black. She was well aware that he usually got back a quarter of an hour after her, but she couldn't repress a surge of nameless anger and frustration. She opened the door. A wave of stifling hot air rushed out at her, enveloped her, and at once she was dripping with perspiration. Her body which had remained cool and dry throughout the day now streamed with sweat. Filled with resentment, she went inside and opened the window and then the door to the balcony. The balcony was covered with grimy leaves, and faintly she recalled last night's autumn wind and rain.

She began washing the rice, muttering fiercely to herself. Her breathing grew faster. She waited impatiently but there was no sign of him. She knew full well that he wouldn't be back for another ten minutes, but her impatience increased anyway. Malicious speculations filled her mind; as her agitation grew her eyes were becoming rimmed in red. Five minutes and he would be home. But at this point, she suddenly hoped that he would be late—ten minutes late, or twenty minutes, or even more. In that case, there would be an excuse for her resentment and anger and she could fly off the handle. Unfortunately for her, he was on time. At six o'clock precisely came the sound of his key turning the lock. She felt almost disappointed, and the flames of fury in her mind raged more and more fiercely. With a great effort, and, it must be said, painfully, she brought herself under control.

The door was pushed open. In order to avoid extinguishing the flame on the gas stove (which stood beside the door), he opened the door just a crack. He thrust his head in first, his face beaming with an amiable, dull-witted smile, and then slowly squeezed himself inside, but she was already beside herself with rage.

"Hurry up! The stove'll go out!"

He quickly pressed his way in and closed the door behind him. The door closed so rapidly, however, that it raised a draft. The tiny points of flame struggled and then one by one went out. She felt a sudden surge of excitement, then, like a river in flood breaching its dikes, and she unleashed a torrent of criticism and complaint.

He dodged hastily into the room, but she became even angrier, the spatula making unnecessarily loud noises in the iron wok. She continued to pour out her complaints, more in explanation to herself than to vent her wrath on him. She had to find an adequate excuse for her attack, or she'd be the loser; but, impartially, she'd already judged from the start that she'd lose. Finally, although he was a patient man, he couldn't keep from breaking in.

"All right, all right," he said, in a conciliatory tone which nevertheless revealed a certain disgust and indifference—irritating her even more. She also felt aggrieved.

She'd often thought that if he were to explode—to show that he was prepared to fight it out with her—she'd probably calm down, but he was always forebearing. During intervals of peace between them, she'd even expressed this wish to him, but he'd never been brave enough to try it. So her theory could never be tested and she continued to be perpetually disappointed in him. With no one to help her restrain herself, control herself, her irritability and nervous tension became completely unmanageable. It was odious and she found herself odious: sick and tired of herself, she was still unable to change, unable to find a solution.

In order to prove that there were grounds for her odiousness, that the responsibility did not lie with her, she redoubled her long-winded defense. Against a background of sizzling oil the room filled with her nagging, but fortunately his nerves were extremely strong, so strong that he was almost wooden.

He bore everything in silence. Seeing his silent forebearance and prudent caution, she felt sorry for him but even sorrier for herself. Frustrated, humiliated by having become like this, she even experienced a desire to change.

But he already knew her inside out—there was nothing to hide from him! This was what she was like now. Yes, this was what she was like! Then so be it, so be it! Her eyes filled with tears and her heart raged fiercely. But no one could hear her rage—only her nagging, her nagging which not only destroyed his evening but hers as well.

Little by little she became tired, and gradually another hope arose in her, a hope that he'd come and comfort her; she needed tenderness and comforting so that she could rest and recover herself. But there was nothing. Already the veteran of a hundred battles and a hundred setbacks, he had become deaf to her nagging. He had to be insensitive; he had to seal his eyes and ears—all his senses—in order to protect himself so that he could prepare for the next surprise attack and steadfastly and slowly continue his gloriously ordinary existence.

And so they struggled on, each of them alone under

one roof. On the brink of outright warfare but also far away from each other, they were unable to offer each other the slightest help.

Afterwards they had dinner. After this scene, both of them had an excellent appetite, and, later, both were in the mood to watch TV. She'd finally calmed down, and once she'd calmed down, the room became silent and still except for the clear, crisp reverberating voice of the TV announcer.

Despite their tedium and disgust, neither got up and walked out of their cramped lodgings in search of private happiness. It was as if they were bound together and could only be together, for better or worse. And so they carried on, moving around in the small, dim room lit only by a desk lamp. One was propped up on the bed and the other sat in a chair; he read a book and she read the evening paper, and then he read the evening paper and she read a book. The TV stayed on all the time. It was showing a sentimental melodrama which they weren't really watching; it was only on to liven up the place a little. Otherwise, the room was too desolate.

When she'd calmed down completely, she started thinking about Lushan, and at this point she even became quite cheerful. After her storm of anger, her mind was exceptionally clear and mild; she also felt a little guilty. She now told him the news of her assignment. He asked when she was to leave and she answered that it would be in five days. In this way they started talking, peacefully and amicably. He also sat down on the bed, and at last she was able to lean against him and absorb the warmth she had been yearning for.

She was now boundlessly warm and comfortable. He

caressed her as if she were a stray kitten, while she repaid him with small, gentle movements. They felt extremely fortunate and meritorious, and both the day's fatigue and their recent agitation were put to rest. They put aside the unhappiness of both past and future; they simply enjoyed the happiness of the moment. It was only by absorbing energy from the brief happiness of the moment that they could cope with the long and tedious life before them.

She felt sleepy, he felt sleepy too, and they fell into a deep slumber. While they were asleep, they unconsciously parted, lying on their separate sides of the bed until daybreak. The dawn light trickled in through the cracks in the bamboo curtain, gradually weaving a net of brightness which covered the room. Finally, the sun also arrived.

She got up, first sitting on the edge of the bed. The wind blew at the curtain, shifting the sunlight; his body lay in darkness one minute and bathed in light the next. At last, he made an abrupt movement with his limbs, dogpaddling, and sat up crosslegged. They looked at each other blankly: last night's fury and passion had vanished without a trace, like a dream.

Five days later, it was finally time for her to depart. She was taking the 8 p.m. express train and had a second-class sleeping berth. That day, she didn't go to work and slept in late. After he got up, she fell back into a drowsy sleep again. She even had a long dream, but when she woke up she couldn't remember any of it.

When she opened her eyes, the sun had penetrated the bamboo curtain and climbed up the bed. She saw far off that there was a note for her on the bedside cabinet but she was too lazy to reach for it. She was very relaxed and comfortable and didn't want to move an inch. How nice it is to sleep, she thought. She slowly moved her arms and legs; they enjoyed how cool and smooth the bamboo sleeping-mat felt, and she continued to move them back and forth.

She would have liked to go back to sleep, but she'd slept enough and couldn't sleep any longer; her eyes wouldn't even close tight. Through her half-opened eyes, she saw the inverted shadow of her own eyelashes, and looking past that shadow, she slowly shifted her gaze at random: the top of the wardrobe was piled high with newspapers, and the newspapers were covered in dust; dust was flying in the sunlight, and the sunlight made it shine. On the door to the balcony hung a pot of once-splendid orchids. They were all dead, except for a few leaves which looked like shallots. Their shadows happened to fall on the dressing table. On the dressing table was an electric shaver, still plugged into the socket, it hadn't been pulled out. It dimly occurred to her that just now there'd been a sudden noise, and she felt like shouting something at the noise. In front of the door were his slippers lying where he'd thrown them, and on the stove was a pot. . . .

Her gaze traveled around the room and returned to the bedside cabinet, where a note sat held down by her watch. Gathering up some energy, she stretched out a hand for it. The note said that he'd bought some steamed buns and put them in the pot on the stove, and that he'd ask for time off this afternoon to come back home and give her a hand.

She smiled, stretched languidly and turned over, lying

on her stomach in an extremely comfortable but also terribly inelegant position. Suddenly she felt a disinclination to leave: why should she? Everything was just fine at home, wasn't it: why should she go to all the bother of traveling? Crowded in on a train all night, having to look for the publishers when she got off the train, having to deal with the publishers once she'd found them—not to mention that she'd have to find a hotel.

She suddenly became worried: where would she stay tomorrow night? She hadn't the least idea. Without any help, she'd have to run around a strange town all alone. She was a little rueful now, but time was pressing and she still had much to do—there was her packing, and so on and so forth. Oh dear, what a bore!

At this point, the various ways in which her husband would be better off occurred to her: she wouldn't be having a good time—she'd be leaving him safe at home for ten days—and she'd return even more exhausted! She felt extremely tired; and time was getting very short. She got up in a rush and busied herself finishing all her chores. It wasn't yet noon, but she started to get a little anxious. She waited, worrying, for the day to come to a close and for the time of her departure, and as she waited she began to almost panic.

As evening came, her anxiety left her exhausted. Then, unaccountably, a sense of boredom came over her, and she became irritable again. An unreasonable rage rose within her, and on the most petty grounds she launched into a lengthy enumeration of his wrongdoings. Despite his long experience with her moods, he couldn't help getting depressed. He lowered his head and drank in silence. She set out her woes like a tray of hors d'oeuvres, her head covered with rollers. These rollers were a blaze of different colors, brilliant purples and reds, giving her an air of confused vivacity.

Finally, coming to the end of his patience, he raised his head.

"All right, all right," he said, after several false starts. "You're about to leave. I don't want to start a fight."

He lowered his head again and went back to his drink. This statement, she didn't know why, brought her to a halt. She could have replied, "You mean you would've started a fight if I weren't leaving? And just what grounds, I'd like to know, would you have for starting a fight!" Continuing along these lines would have provided her with a new topic to start on—in fact, she could have gone on endlessly. But she kept silent, and refrained from any vigorous reply. He sensed something strange about her passivity, and unconsciously raised his head again. They looked at each other in silence. Then they lowered their heads and returned to their meal, her grievances at an end.

For a long time afterwards, she often, often remembered that evening—how at their last meal together before she left, he deliberately, in order to beat a retreat, made this statement:

All right, all right.

You're about to leave.

I don't want to start a fight.

In the days that followed, each of these short sentences became a kind of omen. But at this point, neither knew it. They only experienced a faint, very faint, uneasiness. Why were they uneasy? When she tried to work it out, the uneasiness disappeared, slipping beyond her grasp.

After that she calmed down, and without further incident they remained on good terms until she boarded her train. As the train was about to depart, after the bell had started to ring, she suddenly recalled that she had something to tell him. She flung up the window, stuck her head out and told him that the spareribs and pork in the refrigerator had to be taken out to defrost for two or three hours, so he should come back home during his lunch break and take the meat out, and he should remember to put it in a dish or the melting ice would overflow everywhere. . . .

The bell was ringing and he couldn't hear clearly, so she had to repeat every sentence two or three times. Before she'd finished, the bell stopped and the train began to move. He walked alongside the moving train, his walk gradually breaking into a run.

Holding on to the window frame, she thrust her head out in a valiant attempt to finish what she was saying, but the distance between them increased as the train picked up speed. The wind whistled past her ears, so that she couldn't even hear her own voice. He was still doing his best to keep up, however, and she yelled at him to stop. Seeing her lips move, he became even more convinced that she was trying to tell him something important and redoubled his efforts.

The train increased its speed and despite his efforts he was soon left behind, becoming a smaller and smaller moving black spot. She suddenly felt a little forlorn, and tears welled up in her eyes. The train left the brightly lit station and entered fields shrouded by night. She was still leaning out of the window, looking back. She saw the end of the train snaking at high speed through the dark countryside. The rice paddies along the tracks gleamed dimly and lights twinkled on the far distant horizon. The moon had risen, glowing in the sky. She saw the pale shadow of the train in the moonlight, snaking through the vast space between heaven and earth.

What had he been running for! There'd been nothing particularly important, she thought, holding back the warm tears in her eyes; she could write after she arrived. Why was it necessary to speak just then! She was dimly aware, however, that what she wanted to say was not what she had actually said, nor, for that matter, anything else she might have said: what was said was secondary. When the bell rang, suddenly she'd felt an unaccountable sense of urgency: she had to say something to him—if she didn't speak now, then it would be too late.

Why should it be too late? She still didn't understand. Because the bell had rung, and as soon as the bell stopped, the train would start to move, and as soon as the train moved, she'd be on her way and he'd be left behind. It was then she had urgently wanted to speak to him, and she'd racked her brains for something to say. Yes, she'd thought, what could she say? It seemed she was so flurried she couldn't think of anything, and then it suddenly occurred to her that the pork in the refrigerator needed defrosting and she'd started to speak, competing against the sound of the bell. Oh, that insistent bell—it was as if it tolled a true parting. An odd suspicion plagued her mind.

This suspicion continued to preoccupy her until it

became an irritation, so she took a novel from her bag and started to read. After reading for a while she felt tired, so she stood up, made the bed, and went to sleep. As she nodded off, still half awake, she fell into dreaming. The dreams swayed in rhythm with the train and were filled with "clackety-clack" sounds. She slept the sleep of the exhausted. Mixed with night fog, a draft blew over her, cold and moist; black specks of coal smoke stuck to her body, and she felt clammy. In one dream she took a bath and even washed her hair, feeling pleasantly refreshed, but even then she felt a persistent sense of regret, perhaps because she was aware that this was only a dream. When she finally did arrive at her hotel and was giving herself a thorough scrub in the bathroom, she suddenly recalled this dream. As a general rule she never remembered dreams.

The people attending the conference first assembled at the provincial capital; they were to set off for Lushan the next day. Almost all the writers had arrived, apart from two who were due on an evening flight. As for the constant stream of editors and journalists pouring in from all directions, the organizers of the conference had entirely declined to be responsible for arranging their lodgings, but she was in luck. It just so happened that there was a spare bed in the rooms assigned to the women writers, and they squeezed her in there. The other editors and journalists were put up in hotels in the vicinity (though they weren't actually very near) or else went directly on to Lushan to wait there.

Nothing could have been more convenient for her, meeting the writers day and night. Although it wouldn't have been proper to openly solicit manuscripts and upset the publishers who'd organized the conference, she did take the opportunity to make friendly contacts with the writers with a view to their future work. Besides, she was so attractive in appearance, so adept in conversation, and so tactful in her behavior that she created a very good impression on people.

It was a very busy time for the hosts: there were people to be met, and when they'd been met there were accommodations to be seen to, and there were also of course courtesies to be exchanged. And although they were only staying the one night, the writers could not be left without entertainment, so tickets were purchased for a song and dance performance. The writers, however, wanted to see the local Jiangxi opera. After protracted enquiries, it was discovered that only a small out-of-town troupe was performing that night. Again tickets were purchased, but one of the writers had developed a fever after his journey while the rest by then had lost interest. The hosts were so busy and things were in such confusion that they were obliged to turn to her: she was asked to accompany one of the directors to the airport to meet the two writers. She was happy to agree.

What with everything having turned out unexpectedly well, and refreshed from her long bath, she was in very good spirits, full of energy, and completely relaxed. She kept thinking: it really was right to have made the trip. What it would have been like if she hadn't come, she simply didn't care to think.

She didn't put her newly washed hair in rollers—that would have looked ugly and ridiculous. She just dried her hair with a towel, combed it out, and gathered it in a rubber band behind her neck. The effect was inadvertently quite charming. Then she changed into a sleeveless dress cut on the bias and put on a pair of rope sandals. She looked very young and very fresh.

Shortly after dinner, she was collected for the trip to the airport.

She and Mr. Yao, vice-president of the literature and art section of the publishers, were driven to the airport in a car. On the way they chatted about the plight of publishing, various fortunate developments and changes in fiction writing, and exchanged gossip about the characters and fortunes of the two writers who were arriving on Flight 1157. Mr. Yao also pointed out the local tourist attractions they passed in the car. Without noticing, they had arrived at the airport. There was still nearly an hour before the flight landed, so they sat down to wait. After some time had passed, they felt concerned, and she went to the information desk to inquire. Assured that the flight was not overdue, she stopped worrying and returned to the sofa, where they continued to wait and chat.

The driver, who was extremely resourceful, had located through various roundabout ways an old friend, and was able to drive them directly onto the airfield to meet their visitors.

The airport was vast, so vast it seemed boundless and yet close to the sky. It was cloudy, with no stars and no moon. In the distance, dim and indistinct, stood several airplanes, like big, motionless birds, while beetle-like trucks shuttled back and forth without a sound. The place was deserted except for the wind which swept along the tarmac, wrapping itself round their ankles.

Standing there, they felt at a loss, not knowing in which direction to move. The airport was so empty, the sky hung just over their heads; they stood uncertainly between the vast sky and the vast land. They seemed hypnotized by the sensation of uncertainty, and neither spoke. They stood there silently, and felt they had already been standing there for a long time. The sky blanketed them and seemed very near and at the same time very far away.

At this point, someone told them that the airplane in front of them was the flight they were to meet. They walked towards it.

It was a very small aircraft, almost completely lost in the darkness. Walking through the curtains of the night, they caught full sight of the plane. People were emerging from the door over the landing stairs, which were only five or six steps high. They stepped down onto the lower treads, reached the ground and walked slowly towards them, carrying an assortment of large and small bags. A luggage truck had stopped at one side, silently waiting for the baggage to be unloaded.

As she walked slowly forward, Yao suddenly halted at her side, and then came the sound of hearty greetings, the short phrases swiftly scattering and becoming lost in the vast airfield. She stopped short and turned and in front of her stood two middle-aged men of about the same height, one with glasses and the other without.

Yao made the introductions. They smiled at her, affable and friendly. The one with glasses stretched out his hand, a big warm hand, and shook hers, which was a little cold. Then the one without glasses also stretched out his hand. Their hands, however, didn't meet smoothly. As soon as their fingertips touched, they both became a little flustered. Their hands sprang apart and then tried to find each other a second time, but failed again. When they finally managed to shake hands properly, both felt a bit uncomfortable. Half-consciously, she was slightly upset by the incident—the whole day had gone so easily up to this point. A long time afterwards, she realized that what had happened was memorable. At this moment, however, only aware that she seemed to have made a fool of herself, she felt depressed.

She turned around and walked with them to the terminal. When she turned, stars suddenly appeared in the sky—stars which peered out from behind the clouds and looked down over the earth. The stars were so near, but as soon as she raised her head towards them, they became distant. The airport looked even more vast in the starlight, creating a sense of ineffable desolation.

They walked together toward the lighted area, entered the terminal and waited for the luggage to arrive— there was only a small, black vinyl suitcase to come, belonging to the man with glasses.

"Where's yours?" she asked the man without glasses.

He patted the orange carry-on bag over his shoulder (the kind with four wheels on its underside) and didn't speak.

The talking was left to the man with glasses, who chatted away in great good humor, even clapping Yao on the shoulder. Beside him, Yao's slight figure looked even slighter and more ordinary.

He, however, just stood to one side, listening with a tolerant smile, with his bag still on his shoulder. Taking hold of the back strap, she suggested putting it down while they were waiting, since the baggage would take some time to arrive. He held the strap at the front, and between the two of them they lowered the bag to the ground. As they straightened up again, they exchanged a smile as if they'd reached a kind of understanding.

Somewhat embarrassed, she turned aside and listened attentively to the other writer's witticisms. He was talking about an odd encounter which took place just before they boarded the plane. When he got to the point of the story, she burst out laughing. She sensed that he was also listening attentively and felt pleased; she even felt there was nothing in the world that could trouble her now. How delightful it was! She turned slightly to face the terminal's open windows as a breeze drifted in, and she saw the stars, a whole skyful of stars.

When the luggage appeared, the driver took the writer with glasses to claim his suitcase, while Yao, she, and he stayed where they were, in front of the big window facing the parking lot, the soft breeze caressing their backs. Yao, apparently worn out by his social efforts, had temporarily run out of things to say. She didn't feel inclined to talk either, however, and remained silent, and as he was by nature not talkative, a hush fell over them.

She sensed that Yao was sending her an imploring glance, but she didn't feel like talking. She found the silence wholly natural, not in the least awkward—even meaningful. Yao's forced pleasantries, on the other hand, seemed superfluous and clumsy—and in the end, a little disconcerted, he shut up. The three of them then contented themselves with exchanging friendly glances and smiling cheerfully.

High up behind him she saw an enormous clock, the hands pointing at a quarter past nine precisely. She gazed at it for a long time, she looked at this quarter past nine for an age, and only lowered her gaze when the minute hand made its almost imperceptible move.

At this point, the two men had collected the suitcase, calling out "Let's go!" to them.

"Let's go," she echoed, too, and bent over to pull his orange bag from the floor. Not wanting to let her take it, he also grabbed the strap, but she wouldn't relinquish her side, and they both stood there, refusing to yield. Finally, with his free hand, he seized her fist which was pulling at the strap and removed it from the bag. His hand was extremely big and completely enclosed hers. Her hand in his hand suddenly became small, and seemingly childlike. A little disconcerted, she was obliged to give way, and then they walked in parade order through the whole huge terminal, passing under the big clock.

They got in the car, the writer with glasses sitting beside the driver. He, she, and Yao sat in the back, with her in the middle. He asked her if he could smoke. She didn't answer, but stretched out her hand to open the ashtray on his side. He lit a cigarette. The smoke drifted past her cheek, and like a breeze ruffled her hair. Unexpectedly, she felt moved, and tears welled up in her eyes.

Suddenly she gave a deep sigh. She felt extremely happy. After only one evening, everything had abruptly changed shape—not only in her life, but also in herself. What had happened to her former anxiety, tension, and disgust? All had disappeared like smoke, as if they had never existed. Her mind was clear as a tranquil pool.

She sighed abruptly, and Yao turned to look at her in

surprise. She felt a sudden surge of shame, and rued
being so complacent as to forget herself. But he didn't
turn his head; he showed no surprise, as if he understood. She couldn't help turning a little to look at him.
He was stubbing out his cigarette in the small ashtray,
and she saw his neck connected with the line of his jaw.
She thought about his novels that she'd read. The novels
suddenly became intimate, and also somewhat myste-
rious.

The car sped along the dark road, and the shadows of
trees on both sides swept over them. She leant back in
her seat, looking past his shoulder at the dark objects
outside the window, her mind full of dreams and fancies.
The lights gradually became more frequent and then
dense as the car entered the urban area, passing along
Jinggangshan Avenue, the local equivalent of Beijing's
Changan Avenue. The August First Uprising monument
loomed tall and silent, a bright star at its topmost peak.
The star was not illuminated but glowed with a gathered
light as if it were completely transparent. The car slowed
down and merged with the river of traffic.

Tomorrow they would go to Lushan, she informed
him. He listened, pleased. At Lushan it was cool and
fresh, she added, as if she were the host. She also men-
tioned that the weather was still very warm although
autumn, according to the calendar, had begun some time
ago.

"One of the ovens, isn't it!" he remarked.

"It's much better at Lushan," she replied. "You need a
sweater in the mornings and evenings. You should be
careful," she added, glancing across at him.

He was wearing a short-sleeved sports shirt and

shorts; stretching from the high-cut shorts his legs were covered with curly black hair. She averted her eyes as if a little disgusted.

He replied that he'd brought a windbreaker, and pointed behind them at his traveling bag in the trunk. At this point, Yao, who seemed to have recovered, began to tell stories about Lushan; without pausing between one and the next, he related a number of tales.

When the car stopped in front of the hotel and they clambered out, he revealed that he'd purposely borrowed *Tales of Lushan.* Yao had already gone to the back of the car and was busying himself collecting their bags, so he didn't hear this. Only she heard, and she gave him a smile. He smiled back, and they again felt that there was an understanding between them.

It was eleven o'clock when she got back to her room, and her roommate, a young girlish-looking writer, was fast asleep. Afraid of disturbing her, she didn't turn on the light. The moon shone in through the thin curtain, and by its light she went quietly to bed.

She lay on her back, reached out her legs and then stretched her arms very straight. Her outstretched body was very comfortable, and very beautiful. Moonlight bathed her long slender form. She measured herself carefully through half-closed eyes, and touched by her softness and beauty, she felt a lump in her throat. She relaxed, curled up her beloved body, and snuggling under the clean, crisp quilt, started to look back on her eventful day. She began to examine her actions and manner during the course of this day, like a student reviewing her conduct. The result was satisfactory, except for that inexplicable long sigh in the car, when somehow

she'd forgotten herself. She felt inwardly a little depressed, but anyway, in spite of that, it had been a very
good day, and she had many more good days, perhaps
even better than this, before her. She would spend these
days in the best possible way, and be free of any regret
afterwards. She almost fancied that the ten-day conference would never end, that the days would last
forever—that these ten days were a kind of eternity.
Stimulated but calm, she fell asleep. In her dreams she
took a train again, clickety-clack, clickety-clack, the train
ran on without ever stopping, passing between an enormous sweep of sky and a huge expanse of earth, drawing
a long shadow behind it, and sometimes ringing its bell.

The next day, at five in the afternoon, they arrived at
Lushan. They checked in at a resthouse which looked
like a holiday villa, facing a clear, green lake with a vast,
indistinct mountain range beyond.

By this time editors and journalists from all over the
country had arrived in swarms. Here, the publishing
house was powerless to seal off the writers, and competi-
tors were pretty much allowed to do as they pleased. The
organizers, however, were naturally a little jealous and
were constantly on their guard against any possible leak
of manuscripts into others' hands. For them to pay the
bills while others feasted at the banquet would have been
like sewing another's trousseau!

She was the only one they didn't take precautions
against. When they were together she was regarded as
one of them. She was also very sensible and tactful, never
mentioning manuscripts to the writers. In fact, at this
point, she was reluctant to think about manuscripts. To

commission them, to read them, to send them to the press, to correct the proofs one by one—all these things seemed to be far away, even further away than her previous existence. She was no longer even the same person that she was before. She seemed to have totally changed, and her state of mind was completely different. She'd become serene and composed. Without realizing it, she'd found a way of controlling herself, and this control made her happy: it became the purpose of her daily life in this new world. She had a strong desire to be a tranquil person, and as a tranquil person bring unalloyed delight both to others and to herself. She sensed that the people around her had formed a good impression of her; wished to be with her; would not forget her in whatever they were doing; and would miss her if she weren't there. She was extremely grateful for this, and felt that life was becoming truly beautiful.

At dusk, fog poured in from the other side of the mountains like an avalanche. The lake disappeared within only a few seconds, becoming an enigma hidden in a vast sea of mist. The mountain range was also inundated by a sea of fog, leaving only the tapered peaks rising above like isolated islands in the ocean. Like a ghost, the sun descended indistinctly through the fog, which continued to spread with a faint whistling sound. Everyone crowded onto the balconies, leaning over the railings and gazing into the distance at the dense white fog, as it rolled in with its hint of whistling. Like water casting off terrestrial gravity, the fog flowed in all directions. At times it would reveal a little of the true face of the mountains but then swiftly conceal it, so that this true face became an illusion.

Feeling the damp, cool air everyone had put on colorful sweaters and jackets, but no one had expected the fog to roll in so soon, to thread its way through them, to flow back and forth, and to penetrate between them no matter how closely they huddled together. Even if they were holding hands, the fog threaded its way though the chinks between their fingers to separate them. Gradually the sound of people talking became indistinct, and what was apparently nearby sounded as if it came from a distance. Their figures also became blurred. The fog wound around you, me, and him, like the sea making its way among reefs.

Under cover of the fog, people became even more unrestrained, all speaking at once, loudly and excitedly, so that nobody could hear anyone else, only themselves. As the mist sealed everyone off into separate and distinct entities, they shouted descriptions of the shape of the fog before them, trying to pass on the news that for an instant the mountain was revealed, but nothing could be communicated, and each was left intoxicated with his or her own scene.

She didn't speak. The feeling of unrestrained indulgence had the opposite effect on her, making her extraordinarily calm. In fact, the fog-shrouded scenery could only be appreciated in peace and quiet; the landscape covered with mist was in harmony with a world without words. She leant calmly against the railing, undisturbed by the noise around her. She had never been as tolerant and generous as at this moment. In addition, in her calm mood, she sensed that he was also quiet; she even felt empathy with his silence and his communion with the mountain, while at the same time, her empathy was also gradually, little by little, accepted by him.

She and he stood there with two other people between them, not exchanging a single glance, still and quiet amid the excitement and noise. They noticed each other because of their common silence, and felt at home with each other's wordlessness. At this moment, they felt that they'd begun a conversation—no, they'd been in conversation all the time. They'd transmitted messages when they'd had no intention of transmitting anything; they'd transmitted a message about the mountain behind its barrier of fog, a message about the lake, and a message about themselves behind the same barrier of fog. Among the crowd of people trying to shout each other down, it was only this wordless pair who talked to each other. Complementing each other, they'd truly helped themselves, and comprehended the landscape. Their effortless empathy and achievement far surpassed any excited and restless onlooker.

She was deeply proud of her silence, deeply proud of being able to understand the landscape, and even more deeply proud that only she and he understood it through their silence. But with a slight shiver she also felt a little restless and confused. She even felt indistinctly that something was about to happen. She felt vaguely afraid of it, and also vaguely excited. She also felt obscurely that all this seemed to have been predestined several decades ago, that it was innate in her, that it shared a common existence with this setting, that it was fate, that it was nature, and that since it was inescapable anyway, she had no intention of trying to escape.

But nothing happened.

The light was fading. Exhilarated, they slowly went downstairs to dinner. The three famous products of Lushan were served at dinner: rock frog, which looks like field frog but is plumper and more tender; rock fungus, which looks like wood fungus but is more nutritious; and rock whitebait, which looks like ordinary whitebait but is more expensive. She and he sat at two tables. She sat at the east table facing west and he sat at the west table facing east, so that they sat facing each other from a distance, separated by the space of two whole tables.

She turned her head to look out the window. Directly outside the window was a rough path leading up the mountain. There were no steps to this path; adventurous people had beaten it out from the welter of shrubs and rocks. In the dim twilight two figures came limping down the path, water bottles hanging around their necks and sticks in their hands. They'd rolled their trouser legs up to the knee and their calves were scratched and bloody. After stumbling down the path, they walked around the front of the courtyard to the main road. This road, which was paved, wound along the valley in meandering bends and zigzags.

She heard a clock striking from a long way off—she heard it strike but she couldn't count how many times. She wasn't wearing her watch; she'd forgotten it when she'd washed her face a moment ago and set it down by the sink. So she'd forgotten it—it didn't matter. Time didn't seem necessary here; time had lost its significance. Here day and night, sunrise and sunset—these were all that were wanted.

It was getting dark. The lights came on, swaying uncertainly in the fog. She gazed at the brightest light, swaying in rhythm with it, chasing it with her eyes until it gradually came into them, and from her eyes into her heart. Then her heart leapt from her body into the distant fog, where it shone with a dim glow.

Suddenly, she gave an abrupt start and turned her head. A new dish had been placed on the table; steam wafted up from it. The clock was striking the hour, long and slow. She realized that this long spiritual journey had actually taken place within the space of only a moment, and was moved without quite knowing why. Two tables away, across a barrier of two rows of shoulders, he was smoking. The smoke curled upwards. It reached her through the warm, greasy air; it hadn't been polluted, but retained its bitter freshness. With her own heart she felt the wordless and unseeing attention of another heart. She moved in this attention. Because of it, her every action had meaning. In this instant, her life possessed a new ideal.

After dinner there was a dance. The dance was to be held in the dining hall one hour after the meal. Leaving the table, she went back to her room and locked herself in the bathroom. She stood there facing the mirror for a long time, and for a long time observed her figure in the mirror. The self in the mirror gazed at her as if she were another being. She seemed to have a lot to say, and although in the end nothing was said, she understood instinctively what she meant. She turned her face slightly and without being conscious of what she was doing examined herself from different angles. Suddenly she felt that she was estranged from the self in the mirror, as if she did not recognize her but needed to become reacquainted with her, to study her, and get close to her. She still couldn't recognize herself clearly. She had become very strange, very remote, but at the same time strangely familiar.

After looking in the mirror for quite a while, she pushed open the door and went out. She didn't know how long she'd been in there. There was no one in the room, just as when she went in. Her roommate, the young woman writer, hadn't returned, or perhaps had come back and gone out again.

She lay down on the bed, and closed her eyes to rest. The day had actually been very tiring, but she didn't feel at all weary. Closing her eyes, she felt them moving restlessly under her eyelids. It was so quiet in the room that she felt a little uneasy. There was no sound of people at all, as if everyone in the whole building had disappeared. She lay there quietly, attentively. She heard the sound of rushing water outside the window. Was it raining?

She propped herself up and looked out of the window—total darkness. Nothing could be seen: there was only the sound of water enveloping everything. She thought for a moment, stood up, and walked over to the balcony. A half moon illuminated the fog which rose dimly on one side of the lake. There was a sound of splashing water: it came from a spring on the mountainside, rushing into a stream. From under the shelter of trees, its echo reverberated through the valley. Listening to the stream, she was still a little uneasy. She felt she was waiting for something. She was waiting for the dance to start, she explained to herself, and concentrated her whole mind on waiting for the dance to start. She began to feel anxious, however, as if she couldn't wait any longer, unnecessarily anxious. Then, refusing to let herself be anxious, she lay down on the bed once again. Under her eyelids her eyes leapt about, their restless movement making her heart beat faster. At this moment, dimly, she seemed to hear faintly the graceful undulations of a waltz tune—she couldn't lie still a moment longer. She picked up a jacket and went out, draping it over her shoulders.

The corridor was unusually quiet, as if everyone had made a pact to avoid her. Feeling wronged, a little angry, she became more arrogant. She walked slowly along the corridor towards the staircase and leisurely descended the stairs. The door to the dining hall was closed, but the lights were blazing, and the shadows of people inside flickered across the glass-panelled door. Music was playing, not a waltz but a quickstep. The melody seemed to quicken the blood in her veins, and her whole body immediately became alive. Too impatient to wait any longer, she couldn't control her steps but hurried over to the door and pushed it open.

Inside, the hall was almost empty except for a few strangers whirling across the floor—probably the resthouse staff. Bewildered, she didn't know whether to advance or retreat. At that moment, the door behind her was pushed open and their crowd burst in, squealing and shouting. Their noise immediately filled the hall. Her heart finally calmed down, leaving her slightly embarrassed—a little ashamed of her anxiety attack a moment ago.

She saw him, lagging behind the others, smoking as usual.

There were more men than women, so that she had

practically no chance to rest. He didn't approach her for
a dance, however. She had practically a line of dance
partners before her (all the women did, for that matter),
but they hadn't been paired together. As each danced
with another partner, they were sometimes at different
ends of the hall and unable to see each other, sometimes
brushing shoulders as they passed each other by.

Once when she whirled by she almost collided with
him as he too spun around. They raised their heads and
smiled apologetically. Their smiles hinted at a tacit understanding, as if they had a secret pact, a secret between
just the two of them. She felt that her mind was at peace
again, and was extremely happy. She recovered at this
point what she had just lost: she recovered her confidence. His unspoken and unseeing attention, from this
moment on, shone over her again, and she no longer had
to turn and look around. Her mind was at ease. She
devoted herself to dancing, her head slightly back, her
toes executing intricate patterns. She saw a big clock
high up on the south wall, its hands pointing to a certain
time. She couldn't make out the time or even understand
what that time signified. She just gazed at the clock. She
spun past the clock, covertly watching him as he too
circled by it, and many other couples in turn whirled
past.

It was very late when they finally became partners. It
was a quickstep, so quick that their feet hardly touched
the ground. They didn't have time to think but concentrated on dancing, swiftly and tautly following the
rhythm. They didn't even have time to realize that they
could actually slow down by half, just as some relaxed
partners around them were doing. Because they had

started off so fast, they felt they had to continue at the same pace. And now, both of them were somehow afraid of stopping, as if something would happen once they stopped.

The music came to a rapid conclusion, and their hands immediately disengaged. Her palms were sweaty, she didn't know if it was her perspiration, his, or theirs mixed. They parted hastily. He should have thanked her but he didn't say anything. She should have smiled, but she didn't give him a single smile. All of this was to some extent unnatural. Nevertheless, one tune was over and no matter how eventful, how exciting, how full of portents the day had been, it had to have a curtain.

The next day they were to go to the Immortal's Cave.

When the sun rose the next morning, the fog swiftly dispersed. Emerging from the blur, blue mountains, jagged cliffs, strange pines, and twisted cypresses shook themselves free of mist and as if awakening, as if coming to life, revealed themselves. The fog fell like dust; lightly it fell, layer by layer, until it lay underfoot, prostrate on the winding mountain paths. The ground was wet. Crystal-clear drops of water hung on the tips of the grass.

The unfettered, warm, dry sunlight shone on them as they set off for the Immortal's Cave, by way of Brocade Valley. The valley was like a man-made circular stage on which clouds and fog performed their magic, ceaselessly gathering and dispersing, deepening and fading while the valley's peaks, rocks, trees and shrubs assumed bizarre and wonderful shapes.

The sun's burning rays transformed the valley into a

place of dazzling beauty. White clouds drifted past like living creatures, clean, white, and soft. Clouds formed a permanent cover over the deep valley, concealing its true nature and screening its bottomless depths so beautifully and innocently that no one realized that only one slip of the foot spelled certain death. Occasionally, unintentionally, a cloud uncovered one corner, laying bare a profound truth, but it was only for a moment. Before people had time to notice, the cloud covered it over again, spreading its white petal-like fringes, unfolding a joyous camouflage; all that remained behind was a faint doubt.

She walked along the narrow mountain path, winding up the valley level by level. The valley lay further and further below, and she could glimpse the other side. The path they had just passed along was narrow and slanting, a white mark painted on the cliff. Without a break, extending along its whole length, marched an ant-like file. Although it was now autumn and the peak season was over, there were still many tourists at Lushan. The valley grew deeper and deeper. She dared not lift her gaze from her feet on the path, afraid of losing her wits and stepping on the white cloud. The cloud was so enticing that she felt like putting out a hand to stroke it. Her heart trembled and without thinking she pushed out her hand to grab at the cliff-face beside her. The rocky surface made a rough scratch across her palm. The scratch had the effect of steadying her, and she felt a little more secure.

She halted, leaning against the cliff to let the impatient line behind her pass. She took off her white, broad-brimmed sunhat and folding it into a small bundle, put it into her bag. At this moment, she caught another glimpse of the other side of the valley. On the path along which they had passed not long before, crawled an unbroken, variously sized column. With the high cliffs to one side and the deep valley below, it resembled a busy troop of worker-ants. She stood there staring at them, the sun shining on her face, her body sweating.

Suddenly, a hand seized her bag by the shoulder strap, and she gave a start. Seeing that it was him, she felt a quiver of excitement, but she was not in the least surprised: it seemed that she had been waiting for him since early that morning. No, she'd been waiting since yesterday, or even earlier, even before Flight 1157 landed. He had come while she was waiting, as she'd anticipated, so it wasn't unexpected.

He relieved her of the bag and slung it over his shoulder. He didn't have a bag himself: a pack of cigarettes in his pocket was enough for him. With her bag over his shoulder, she was obliged to walk alongside him, they were compelled to move in concert, since there were things in the bag she might want to use at any time—a fan, a face-flannel, not to mention her purse, and so on. So they walked on together.

Understanding her feelings about the valley, he let her walk by the cliff-face and he walked on the open side of the path, separating her from the sheer drop. Just at his feet, a lotus-like cloud was drifting; his feet came in contact with its petals, but he walked on perfectly at ease. She saw tiny, sparkling dewdrops on his shoes.

The sun shone high over the valley. The cloud became transparent, as if it were an illusion, a mirage, exposing one layer after another. Pines and cypresses stretched out their arms; cliffs and boulders reared their heads: they were at home, relaxed and unconstrained, free from human interference.

Under the protection of his wide shoulders, she gradually let her gaze fall, slipping past the strange rocks and twisted trees, coming to rest on a patch of blood-red azaleas deep in the valley. In full bloom, they were inconceivably red, wickedly beautiful. Her gaze was scorched by their color but couldn't tear itself away; it pierced deep into their center and was held there, deep in their burning grasp before it was finally able to wrench itself free, and gradually, laboriously raise itself out of the valley to the withered creepers on the cliff-face. The sunlight peered through for a moment, and then the cloud cover formed again.

He stopped, suddenly wanting a cigarette. She paused too to wait for him. He took out a cigarette from his T-shirt pocket, a very common brand of cigarette, and then took a lighter out of his shorts pocket, one which was not so ordinary: it was a narrow, flat lighter, black with a gold rim. He started to light the cigarette, but a wind blew from the valley and extinguished the flame. He tried again, using more force. The flame flickered, struggled for a while, and went out again. He sheltered the flame from the east, and the wind blew from the west; he blocked it from the west, and the wind blew from the east; he bent over, and the wind blew from below; he straightened up, and the wind blew from above. The wind came from every direction, surrounding him, encircling him; this was the wind of Brocade Valley. He was doomed to be unable to light his cigarette—he was fated not to be able to light it by his own efforts.

Finally, she couldn't bear to watch any longer and stepped forward. She came closer to him until she was standing right in front of him, then cupped her hands around the lighter. The flame wavered inside the walls formed by her hands, and this time it was not extinguished. He dragged on it quickly several times. The cigarette end rapidly glowed, darkened and glowed again, at last it was lit. At that instant, he raised his eyes and looked into hers.

They were very close to each other, he and she, only inches apart. The wind-blown strands of hair across his forehead almost touched hers, and their eyes gazed into each other, only inches apart. Like two silk ribbons floating in the space between them, their glances brushed against each other, collided, joined, knotted, and finally, slowly began to weave a net. Abruptly she let her hands drop, and the flame went out.

Not knowing when or how they began, they were walking again, circling Brocade Valley. They had started to walk without being conscious of it. Brocade Valley was like a trap: no matter how they went, they could not get out. How long this path was! The sun had dried the dew, and the path was very dry, very soft. The cloud in the valley floated back like a stream. They walked through some dry grass, which rustled under their feet.

She averted her face slightly, studying the steep cliff, while he gazed over the valley beside him. Their eyes had shifted apart, drawing on the floating ribbons that connected them but not breaking them. She realized that the event she had long been preparing for was now finally happening. It was as if all the vague premonitions she'd had for many days had found an answer: they had found their source and their refuge. Nevertheless she grew calm. Having at last settled down sufficiently, she turned away from the cliff and looked directly ahead where a sudden burst of noise filled the air. One more bend in the path and they had reached the Immortal's Cave.

When they mounted the steps, the terrace was crowded. Amid the noise and bustle they became confused, barely knowing where they were. They pushed their way over to the stone tables by the balustrade and sat down. Then they saw that most of their people were sitting around tables drinking bittersweet soft drinks made of concentrated essence and saccharin. When they saw them arrive, their friends enthusiastically waved them over and insisted they take their turn standing under a pine tree on the other side of the balustrade to have their photos taken.

For a moment, they had a sense of having returned to the mundane world. Although it was noisy and confusing, and they weren't quite up to coping with the situation with ease, they still felt secure within themselves since there was so much to hold on to. They willingly allowed themselves to be ordered about, and afterwards chatted together with the others, nibbling on tasty melon seeds while he smoked as well.

He still had difficulty lighting his cigarette, but this time she didn't help him. The moment just now when she'd cupped the flame within her hands was so rare and precious that to repeat it even once would be to profane it. It was an act which had a particular meaning for him and for her, one which should be never abused. Any abuse would distort it, make it ordinary, deprive it of meaning and value. It was an act only she and he knew about and understood, an act that belonged only to her and to him. It was a secret.

To sit in a crowd while possessing something entirely private is a great joy, a blessing above all others. She became even more generous and at ease than before, making an even better impression on everyone. No one surpassed her in getting along well with the people in this group, and no one derived more pleasure than she did from them. They each talked to their own friends with great interest, listening attentively to what they were saying, and didn't exchange a single glance with each other. But every single word and every single expression was for the other. It was as if they had devised and kept up a conspiracy, because all the others were excluded from participation—to their great satisfaction.

The sun was fierce, but she didn't want to get her bag back from him and take out her sunhat. She didn't want to have too much contact with him, as if concerned that carelessness on her part would destroy the tacit understanding—still not very firm, even quite fragile— between them. She dared not abuse this understanding, since she treasured it so much. Apparently sharing her feelings, he avoided walking next to her on the way back, although her bag was still hanging over his shoulder, as if protecting him and being protected by him. They walked far apart, each merging with another group, and the Brocade Valley which seemed to be another world was as distant as a dream. The dream lived on in their hearts and was part of their every moment; it constantly renewed itself in them and was renewed by them. To relive the same story with someone at a distance is one of life's supreme joys. Hugging this joy to themselves as they walked along the narrow mountain path, they pressed into the crowd, taking part in the general conversation with apparent abandon. At this point, the others seemed to exist for the sole purpose of serving as a foil for their story.

That afternoon a seminar was held in the resthouse's conference room. Since the subject was always literature, it didn't matter what particular topic was set. The editors and journalists turned up when they got the news and soon occupied all the seats around the room. About three o'clock the writers finally arrived and the seminar began. At first there was the usual silence, which lasted half an hour (neither more nor less), followed by the ordinary delay for the usual displays of modesty (which also took half an hour), and then the discussion slowly got under way.

In the beginning people were reserved, but passions began to rise as they got more and more carried away. A new opinion would be advanced, couched in very pointed terms, but before the speaker had finished another would rise to refute him in terms that were twice as harsh. If you listened carefully, however, you'd find that the latter hadn't actually put forward a view contrary to the former speaker's argument but simply used it as a springboard to advance his own grand theory. More than a dozen different opinions which neither contradicted nor confirmed each other flew back and forth. There was no focus to the debate, no general theme: you said your piece and I said mine. Meanwhile the editors and journalists were busily taking notes, afraid of missing something since every word seemed so significant that any omission would be deeply regretted. She was no exception. These brilliant thoughts made her particularly excited because she was particularly clever, extremely good at understanding and extremely sympathetic, unwilling to be isolated and unwilling to be ordinary. This occasion formed a very sharp contrast to her former insipid life and work.

There were quite a few writers at the seminar whose manuscripts had passed through her hands. She'd corrected misspellings and word choices line by line, designed the layout, checked the illustrations, and sent the manuscripts to the printers. When they came back from the printers, already typeset, she went through them again for typos and dropped copy. . . . Ideas formed into writing, writing separated into sentences, and sentences separated into single characters: this was the final breakdown, in which each individual character in isolation was reduced to meaninglessness. How boring her job had been over these long years—without being aware of it, she'd been engaged in boring work for so many years. Now she felt that something had come alive in her body and in her mind, like a bubbling spring of fresh water. She truly seemed to have become another person.

It really was right to have come to the conference; how miserable she'd have been if she hadn't! At this point she caught sight of him sitting at the end of the long table covered with white cloth. He began to speak. After a few words he lowered his head and lit a cigarette; with it between his lips, he frowned and narrowed his eyes, as if affected by the smoke. A flame had leapt up for a few brief moments before going out. A light also seemed to have gone out in her heart, and she had a sudden feeling of desolation. The magical scenery in miraculous Brocade Valley vanished, disappearing without trace in the noisy smoke-filled room. In his actual, visible presence, their dream-like connection in Brocade Valley was suddenly broken, shattered into fragments so fine and transparent that they vanished away, leaving nothing behind.

Her mind was empty; she didn't even hear what he was saying. Her pen stayed on her notepad, drawing a series of five-pointed stars, forming first one chain and then another. She sensed that he wasn't as carried away as the others. He'd always been unusually restrained in revealing his thoughts and feelings, expressing profound ideas in a minimum of words. She also realized that the others had fallen silent and were concentrating on what he was saying, as if his opinions were of great value. She knew his worth went far beyond the ordinary; she knew full well his worth.

At this moment she felt afraid, afraid that the morning scene in Brocade Valley was no more than an illusion, no more than her imagination. She felt anxious, she wanted to grasp it, to touch it, to feel it, no matter how intangible, how complicated, how confusing, how elusive it was.

She gave a sudden shiver. A loud noise sounded just over her head, followed immediately by a distant echo. Confused, she saw the others getting to their feet, as he finished off his speech with a gesture. It finally occurred to her to look up. On the wall behind her was a big clock; the distant sound was the dinner bell. She raised her head to look at the clock, bewildered, and slowly stood up, following the others out of the conference room. The clock was still striking. She floated along with the crowd, like a lonely island in the sea, impelled forward by the others as if she had no will of her own, getting nearer and nearer.

As before there was a dance after dinner. It got lonely in the evenings in this remote area. As if returning home, the mountains retired early behind their barrier of mist. There was a town called Guling not very far away, but they were from the cities and had come here for the natural scenery, and Guling held no interest for them. In addition, it would be full of tourists wandering around with nowhere to go, whereas at the dance it would be both restful and lively. She didn't particularly want to attend but at the same time she was secretly reluctant not to, and so after wavering for a long time she ended up going. She got there right on time. The dancing had already begun with several melodies, and people had just started to notice her absence when she arrived. As the others whirled around the dance floor, she quietly crossed over to the wall and sat down by a square table. Whenever there was a pause in the music, the murmur of the stream outside would break in, bringing news of the mountains. And then, he walked towards her—yes, there was no doubt about it, he was crossing the room towards her. But someone else was also walking towards her, in front of him; he was obviously half a step too late. When he realized that he was a little too late, he hesitated and was about to retreat. There was nothing for it but to stand up and go to meet him. If she had hesitated even a split-second, he would have retreated. She took half a step forward, obliging him to stay.

It was only after they had moved onto the dance floor and taken a few steps that she became conscious that she was dancing with him, so close to him, so intimate. The normally meaningless conventions between partners suddenly became full of significance and made her pulse beat. She blushed, unable to recall how she and he had reached this stage.

Her feet moved naturally in time with the music. They had fallen into the proper rhythm right from the beginning. But they were by no means old hands on the dance floor, and weren't skillful enough to dance and talk at the same time. They couldn't relax, they couldn't make conversation, but secretly they were glad that they didn't have to talk. Her hands felt his hands, her breath felt his breath; sometimes her leg touched his leg. Her mind became calm again, beside his actual, tangible body. Her eyes looked at a point beyond his shoulder; their eyes no longer exchanged glances. Their communion in Brocade Valley had been their last and also their most sacred communication; both of them were unwilling to corrupt that sacred communion with a commonplace visual exchange.

Avoiding contact they collided; not looking at each other, their eyes met. She suddenly felt his heart trembling; her left hand on his right shoulder, she felt this trembling through her palm. She knew that he was not indifferent—no, not at all.

This dance was to end soon; there was already a sense of finality in the music, as if in a dream. She heard him say something. His mouth was near her ear, but his voice sounded as if it came from very far away: it was clear, but nothing could have been more confused; it was natural, but nothing could have been more awkward. He said that it was stuffy inside and they should go for a walk outside first. The way he spoke was both ordinary and not ordinary; what he said was this: "It's stuffy inside, let's go for a walk outside first."

For quite a long time afterwards, whenever she recalled this sentence, she found that it had had a very strong symbolic meaning:

It's stuffy inside.

Let's go for a walk outside.

First.

It seemed that hestitation was no longer necessary; to refuse would have been unreasonable and unnatural. She picked her coat off the back of her chair, while he took his cigarettes and lighter from the table, and then they went out. Nobody noticed them; people were going in and out all the time without anyone paying any attention.

As they left the room, the door swung closed behind them, abruptly cutting them off from the music and chatter inside. It was extremely quiet in the corridor, and their footsteps rang out clearly on the terrazzo floor. They both felt somewhat awkward in each other's presence, not daring to fall silent or even to slow their steps. Hurrying along, they began to speak rapidly in an attempt to dilute the tense atmosphere with ordinary conversation. They were so awkward that they both began to have doubts, and they were also so nervous, afraid of destroying something. But they didn't dare allow a silence to develop. In desperation they engaged in small talk: how the air inside was stale, but fresh outside; how it was cold at night, but very agreeable; how the spring water was sweet, but could be harmful if taken in excess. They couldn't help repeating themselves, even contradicting themselves; they couldn't take the time to stop and think; they rattled on at great speed, afraid of falling silent.

They were terribly afraid of silence—the whole building was silent, and yet all the lights were blazing. The dance music was left far behind. In this still, empty corridor, where the lights stripped away all refuge, they had to create something to hide in. Their chatter broke into the empty silence, a silence which resembled a strange substance, and they felt the pressure of this substance; the silence was also a kind of low-reverberation sound wave, like a transparent membrane stretching over a body of water. Their conversation disturbed the even surface of the water, and they heard the sound of the membrane being scratched.

Continuing to talk, they stepped out onto the flight of stairs leading up to the resthouse. Suddenly they saw the mountain, the shadow of the mountain hidden behind the mist. In the absence of human interference, the mountain came to life, as if it were speaking. They fell silent; their babble came to an end.

At this moment, they stopped feeling any sense of uneasiness or awkwardness. As darkness enveloped them, they had something to cover themselves with; they weren't naked any longer, they needn't feel ashamed. Also, the mountain had so much understanding of the human heart, and gazed down on them with such keen insight, that there was no further need for evasion. Shedding their pretence, they felt relaxed, liberated, free. They stayed in front of the stairs, not venturing further, not venturing into the mist and the darkness. The time for that hadn't yet come; consciously, in unspoken agreement, they stopped at the foot of the stairs. The mist seemed to enclose another unknown world, and they were not brave enough, or not reckless enough, for the idea of going up into it to occur to either of them.

The stars shone on the highest, most distant peaks, and invisible streams flowed swiftly in conversation with the leaves rustling in the wind.

The sun rose today as it had risen yesterday. She and he, however, were no longer the she and he of yesterday. And so the sun was different too, and rose from somewhere neither in the east nor in the west. From then on—no matter how far away she was from him or by how many steps on this long mountain path they were separated—she still felt secure. As he looked at her, she was constantly aware of the attention of his gaze; she strove, happily and wholeheartedly, to try and improve herself. Life presented new meanings, and as if reborn, she felt that the world was fresh and new; she brimmed with curiosity and vitality.

As she walked down these endless nine hundred and fifty-six steps, each step was for him, and because it was for him, it couldn't tire or bore her: even when she was exhausted she was still full of joy and enthusiasm. Under his fixed gaze, however, she was doubly nervous, afraid that a single slip would reveal her weakness; she carefully protected her image in his mind without being conscious

of doing so. It was an image of perfection, so perfect that
it was unfamiliar even to her. She cherished this new self
for her own sake and also for his. If damaged in any way,
it would harm her, it would harm him, it would harm his
gaze, and it would harm his affection for her.

Ah, so she'd gone as far as the word "affection." This
had happened so long ago that its original appearance
had already grown unfamiliar. As it now flashed across
her mind, she immediately felt a tide of emotion sweep
through her. Nine hundred and fifty-six steps, leading
down one by one: she could hear the waterfall at Triple
Springs; its echo rebounded against the steep cliffs.
Quickening her pace she went down, but under her
protracted, fixed gaze the evenly spaced steps turned
into a level road, an endless road on which they were
lined up like railway cars. In a kind of daze, she stopped
and raised her head to look at the sky, ringed by mountains that framed it like the mouth of a well. They had
already descended into the valley and were plunging
further and further into its depths. She gazed at the
green-clad peaks under the blue sky, but as her eyes
suddenly reverted to the ground under her feet, she
staggered and almost lost her footing. Just as her attention wandered, the even stone steps had suddenly become more precipitous, plunging straight down before
her, and as if the mountain was roaring, the sound of
rushing water filled her ears.

People wound along the stone steps, like a file of ants
on the move. Through them she glimpsed him from
behind; his back conveyed his attention to her. Reas-
sured by his back's concern, she was able to continue her
way down, calmly and steadily. Clearly there were nine

hundred and fifty-six steps, but they looked endless. Equally clearly they were endless, but they numbered nine hundred and fifty-six. She expected nothing from Triple Springs; she didn't believe she would ever reach it. Nevertheless, she had to go on, step by step; she had no alternative but to go on, step by step, as if driven by fate: it was almost a kind of predestination. All she could see was his back, further down the steps; everything else disappeared except for his back flickering in and out of sight as it guided her on her way.

Just as she was about to lose hope, she heard people cheering: cheers for Triple Springs and cheers for the nine hundred and fifty-six steps. She knew then that Triple Springs wasn't far off and only a few of the nine hundred and fifty-six steps remained ahead. Through the dense forest she saw the assembled heads and the gushing springs. Then she saw a vast expanse of white: it was a valley—a valley within a valley. The valley was a bottomless abyss.

Finally she saw a steep cliff and a waterfall flowing quietly down its towering heights. Amid the noisy clamor of the springs, the high waterfall was extraordinarily quiet. But all the tumult in the valley had its source in the waterfall, as it quietly and calmly stirred the whole valley into a crescendo. The noise of the water was almost deafening: you could see people were shouting exultantly, but their mouths were opening and closing without a sound. The water swallowed all fainter sounds, and all sounds became faint in the sound of the water. The waterfall poured down from the azure sky over the three falls and nine cliff ridges, as gentle and soft as a maiden. Its murmur reverberated through the whole valley, as if it were crying without hope and without despair.

She walked down the last step, the nine hundred and fifty-sixth step, and put one foot uncertainly on the slanting rock. She was afraid of sliding off, right down to the edge of the cliff, then over, through that white expanse, and down into those bottomless depths. But her feet clung firmly to the rock, and the rough surface caught at her shoes, holding her as she moved forward step by step, away from the edge of the cliff. She bent, fumbling for a place, and sat down. Here she couldn't see the deep valley, but she could see the cloud over it. The cloud hung in the sky, perfectly still. How could it hang in the sky without anything to lean on? It was like a magic trick, there must be something there for it to lean on hidden from our eyes, just like a magic trick. She panted, her head full of strange fancies.

She noticed their crowd playing games beside a stream at the foot of the cliff, trying to catch a towel which had escaped into the water. As soon as it entered the water it became alive, and swam quickly away like a fish past lots of jutting stones, bends in the stream, and outstretched hands. Their shouts and cheers were drowned out by the sound of water, and she saw only their waving hands and prancing feet. At the foot of the cliff, they seemed so tiny, like children; looking at their tiny figures, she felt that they were far, far away.

He did not join this pursuit but sat on a stone beside the stream and smoked. The leaping water splashed his shoes and clothes, even wetting his hair. He sat facing away from her, and she turned away too, so they were back to back.

They sat with their backs towards each other and conversed.

"You're very calm," he said.

"So are you," she said.

"You blend in very well with the mountain," he said.

"The mountain blends in very well with you," she said.

"You look as if the mountain arranged for you to come," he said.

"The mountain looks as if you arranged for it to be here," she said.

"But the mountain's making a racket," he said.

"There's a racket going on in my mind," she said.

"Mine too," he said.

"It'll be quiet once the racket's over," she said.

"Thanks," he said.

The stream splashed along noisily and dashing against rocks, it set off loud echoes, while high up on the steep cliff, a white brook flowed quietly. Sky covered the secluded valley, and in the azure sky she saw a moon, which shone brightly. It was the moon from yesterday, and also the moon which would come this evening—it was on its way, it had already set off.

Enclosed by the mountain, their bodies shrank. The huge mountain squeezed down on their bodies; their bodies squeezed down on their souls; and their souls, suddenly expanding, broke through their bodily shells, and with nothing else to attach themselves to, clung to the rough cliffs. She could feel her heart suspended inside her body, and then she could feel it exit through the top of her head; it even seemed as if she could catch it in her hand, but she didn't move. She was numb, bereft of all emotion; her heart was free to roam at will, abandoning her.

The sun and moon shone in turn in the sky above the empty valley; she did not know what she had experienced; it was as if tens of thousands of years had passed here. She felt only that in the alternation of sun and moon she had been transformed. One self was in retreat, another self was approaching: she was changing into another person. She was herself, but at the same time no longer herself. Oh God, it was truly miraculous!

Consumed by doubt, she had no way of judging between her new and old selves; she didn't know which was the more authentic. But she liked the new self—the one he had seen. The old self was too old: she was bored by it, she no longer treasured it. With her brand new unfamiliar self, she could experience many brand new, unfamiliar emotions—or, one could say, with her brand new, unfamiliar emotions she discovered and created a brand new, unfamiliar self. In her new self she discovered infinite powers of imagination and creativity: she could penetrate deep into his mind, offer him comfort, become a good influence. By making use of her new identity and with her new self instructing her, she seemed to have been reborn. She was so happy! Oh, she was so lucky: lucky that she came, lucky that he came, lucky that they both came. Oh dear, she was so grateful to him, she loved him so much.

When she got as far as the word "love," she couldn't help quivering like a schoolgirl, and through her back she also sensed his trembling. Their agitation passed through the space between them and met above a rock in the emptiness. At this moment, she felt her heart returning to her body: her heart came back fully laden; her heart came home well-stocked. Her heart had traveled around, and after gathering a full load of happiness, it had returned.

Nevertheless she also felt troubled, a sense of disquiet rising slowly through her happiness. Dimly she felt a disagreeable presentiment, a presentiment that this love was doomed to oblivion. Yet this doomed love grew vigorously, indomitably; without ceasing for a second it put forth branches, buds, and leaves. Yesterday only a seedling, today it was a tree that brushed the sky. Attached to the tree, her new life broke through the earth and rose from the ground. Her rebirth came wholly from her love for him, and she believed that he was also reborn because of his love for her. She could not retreat.

Someone was calling her to have her photo taken as a souvenir; everyone else had had their turn and she was the only one left. With considerable reluctance she slowly walked over. The rock underfoot sloped down, to her dismay, down towards the edge of the cliff. She made her way up step by step, feeling very nervous, as if the valley below the cliff were forcing her. When she reached the stream, she grabbed a projecting rock and leaned against it. With the rock separating her from the cliff, she felt a little more secure.

Her sense of security was soon replaced by embarrassment. The photographer was the art editor of the press, who had the determination and confidence to turn each picture into a cover shot. He also had very high expectations of her, and forcefully demanded a variety of film-star poses from her. Secretly she was flattered, but at the same time acutely embarrassed, because he was there.

His eyes were on the stream and his back was still towards her, but his back knew everything. She had no choice: she was already seated on a rock and couldn't come down. She was obliged to put up patiently with the photographer's manipulations. Her embarrassment made her as shy and naive as a schoolgirl, attracting the attention of passing tourists. However, she couldn't bring herself to enjoy these admiring and appreciative glances. As if under torture, she longed for it to be over. Nothing could have been more attractive than the way she looked now, but she was unaware of this and felt acutely depressed.

At last she was able to free herself from the rock. She felt liberated—she felt brought back to life. Spiritedly she jumped down from the rock and walked towards him; without conscious intent, she walked towards him.

She asked if he'd had his picture taken as well, and he replied that yes, he'd also suffered. When he said "suffered" she immediately understood and started to laugh. He didn't laugh, but regarded her steadily. She became embarrassed by his look, but in a way totally different from her previous feeling; there was a pleasantly fearful quality to this embarrassment. She felt like asking him why he was looking at her that way, then thought it too frivolous and silly, and without further comment, she bent over to pick up a handful of pebbles. She cast them one by one into the stream. The stones silently dropped into the turbulent water and were silently swept away. She sensed his eyes caressing her, and her whole body ran hot and cold.

There were no more pebbles left, but he was still

looking at her. When she plucked up the courage to challenge his gaze, he grinned and asked: "Okay?"

"Okay!" she retorted. The water was deafening, over-poweringly loud, but suddenly it fell silent, so their voices rang out above the noise which filled the valley, and they heard each other very easily, as clear as could be.

This was the most incoherent and at the same time most meaningful, the shortest and at the same time most comprehensive conversation in the world. They seemed to have entrusted each other with everything in the exchange of these few words. When they left Triple Springs and set off on the long march up nine hundred and fifty-six steps, their mood was ineffably pure and transparent. They walked side by side along the narrow mountain path, and when from time to time they were separated by people in front or behind, they would stand to the side to let the others pass, falling further and further behind. The nine hundred and fifty-six steps went straight up, and she soon began to pant. He stretched out his hand to her, and she put out hers. When she'd given him her hand she didn't withdraw it. From then on, they conversed through their hands.

Triple Springs gradually fell behind as step by step they mounted the cliff. Nothing could have been more even than these steps, winding their way up one by one. There was nowhere to pause and rest; it was almost impossible to even catch your breath; you had to climb the whole nine hundred and fifty-six steps in one go. They gradually adjusted their breathing and pace, feeling more relaxed once they'd fallen into a rhythm; they only needed to lift their feet mechanically while their hands concentrated on conversation. It was her turn to ask: "Tired?" "No!" his hand answered. "Thanks!" her hand said gratefully, and his hand replied: "That's all right." Afterwards there was silence, with no further enquiry or exchange.

Approaching middle age, they knew very well how to conserve their emotions, "narrowing the channel to prolong the flow." They well understood that the perfect moment before the opening curtain should be appreciated to the full, and that after the curtain, once all was revealed, it would just be routine. They had both had their share of emotional experiences: their emotions had shaped them and they could also mold their emotions. They had already done battle with their emotions, so that in fact they already knew themselves and their feelings, even though they would never admit it. They had made up their minds to love: to have true, whole-hearted, and single-minded love; to love excluding all else. They knew that to lose one's heart was to lose half of oneself, and they were prepared for sacrifice. Educated, experienced, and widely-read, they knew what human beings should be like and worked towards this goal.

Tragedy appealed to them: tragic drama often kept them from sleeping at night, the terrible details attacking them and binding them as they lay awake, wracked by insomnia to the detriment of their health. Easily captured and made prisoner, they were conscious of an imperfection in their minds—a fault which disrupted their peaceful lives but also added color. They longed for more color in their lives; they were not content with mediocrity. Run of the mill life bored them; they preferred a life out of the ordinary.

Fortunately, they had unusual powers of imagination. They owed their education and profession to their imagination, and their education and profession in turn tempered their imagination, developing and strengthening it. Once given a start it could create a whole world, let alone a minor emotional current; it was simply a matter of professional skills.

They were fully prepared for sacrifice, and for what they considered worthwhile they would not pause to calculate the results or count the costs. They were also fully aware of implications, being extremely perceptive. They would never devalue their sense of hope; they knew that hopes are more beautiful than facts, and that when hope becomes reality life loses its savor. So they conserved their hopes, keeping them always a step ahead of realization. Over the course of time, and without being conscious of it, they had even developed an ability to make facts return to their original status as hopes and ideals. In this way they could always stay fearful, always at fever-pitch, always filled with childish longings— restless and given to wild flights of fancy. And so their true, whole-hearted, and single-minded love would remain safe and protected from a corrupt world.

They were therefore reluctant to force the pace of their conversation; it would only move forward after each stage had been fully explored, as if they'd discovered a mine with limited treasures: they couldn't waste the least amount, they had to wash it with the finest, closest sieve, before they could move forward and excavate further.

However, all of this was in their subconscious: they weren't even aware of it, let alone prepared to admit it. If the day came when they finally had to explain these things, it would truly be their Judgment Day. But theirs would never come; they wouldn't let it come. They were so perceptive as to have an almost instinctive ability to foretell the future; they wouldn't let their Judgment Day come.

Now, with their hands clasped together, this contact was all they needed for mutual whole-hearted reliance. No one could possibly have gathered how tenderly they were bound to each other in reciprocal love and affection at this moment. To other people they were only a man and a woman returning from Triple Springs, carefully helping each other up these nine hundred and fifty-six steps. It was noon, and the sun beat fiercely down on their heads, but they felt nothing: all their feelings were concentrated in their two hands, his right hand and her left.

Finally signs of human habitation came into view at the top of the nine hundred and fifty-six steps. A family had opened a tea-shed there which also served as a café, and its smoke-filled kitchen faced the last step; they knew that their people would be waiting for them inside. When they reached the nine hundred and fifty-fifth step, he mounted the last step first and then pulled her up, so energetically that she collapsed against his chest. Then, very softly, he kissed her on the forehead. Nothing could have been more natural than this kiss—they had actually kissed each other thousands of times in their minds. But this physical kiss formally raised the curtain, and once the curtain was up, there was no possibility of escape, no possibility of change, no possibility of retreat: the performance had begun.

They loosened their hands, which were damp with perspiration, and avoiding further contact, went round the smoke-filled kitchen to the front of the café. As expected, their people were taking up all the seats, halfway through cups of cold tea. Their tea had also been served on the table, and apparently no one had noticed their being late. In fact they were only a few steps behind the others, but the space between these few steps was enough to separate two worlds, two ages.

They sat down and had some tea, which was fresh and sweet, only five cents a cup. A seven year old boy was collecting money and pouring tea, and she spoke to him at length. When she asked him how old he was, his answer gave her a shock—it turned out that he was ten. Then she asked if he went to school and where, if he had brothers or sisters, and so on. She spoke kindly and listened attentively to his answers.

He, meanwhile, was sitting at another table discussing Triple Springs, whether it was true what people often said, "If you haven't been to Triple Springs you haven't been to Lushan." Some people didn't think so, but he came out strongly in favor, giving as his reason that Lushan had been overrun in recent years, and this spot was the only place where its original character was still preserved.

Each talked on his or her own topic to his or her own companions, but in fact they were still talking to each other, carrying out a conversation on each other's topic that was both distant and close. At times their conversation didn't even need to be relevant in content or form. From then on they were in constant communication. Their conversation made all other talk extraordinarily significant, imbued with new interest. Every word she spoke was meant for him, whether he was present or not, and every word he uttered was meant for her, whether she was there or not. At the same time they were quite unaware that their conversation bore a distinct resemblance to the speeches at the seminar, where everyone was very keen on setting forth their own opinions but not in the least interested in other peoples'. They were only engaged by what they were saying and not by what was being said to them. The only exception was if the other person was talking about them, in which case they'd become doubly interested—then they could listen a hundred times over without getting bored, even refusing to listen to anything else. They were only interested in themselves and only paid attention to themselves: their conversation in fact amounted to an internal dialogue, and the other person was no more than a fictitious audience.

For this reason, it was in fact more difficult for them to communicate between themselves than with other people, and they were more distant from each other than from others, because with each other they were only too anxious to express their opinions, whereas with other people, politeness and education restrained them. They constantly attempted conversation and they constantly failed at conversation. However, in spite of all this, they felt mentally replete, mentally exhilarated.

The most real and substantial communication between them was that kiss. She constantly felt it burning on her forehead, burning like a brand in the center of her brow. She dared not touch it with her hand—it might then be noticed, or something might thereby be destroyed. She was at a high pitch of excitement, but at the same time somewhat affectedly melancholy: she would turn the brand into a scarlet A, as in Hawthorne's novel. It was burning hot in a way that excited her.

The brand was also on his lips. When he used his cold tea to cool it, the tea was heated. He felt uneasy; he who had always been self-possessed felt uneasy. He dared not moisten it for fear of burning his tongue, and then also for fear of losing something. He smoked, holding the cigarette in his lips, but he felt that there was a kind of barrier between his lips and the cigarette.

They both seemed numbed, bearing a burden on her forehead and on his lips; it tired them, but in fact they were afraid of losing it and wanted to preserve it carefully. It was only towards the end of that day that they found the chance to slip out of the rest house and enter the dense mist, and as they embraced, melt the brand with a thousand hot kisses, smooth it, and engrave it deep in their hearts.

They embraced in trembling fearfulness, but also with reckless abandon. In fact, they were so deeply hidden by the dense mist that not a single eye could invade their privacy.

When finally they went into the mist, there was indeed another world behind it.

"It was Heaven's blessing that you came to Lushan too," he murmured.

"It was Heaven's blessing that you came to Lushan too," she murmured.

It was Heaven's blessing that they had both come to Lushan: how wonderful to be at Lushan! It had given them so much of what they had both expected and not expected. The mist twined round their arms and legs, slipping between their clinging bodies, finding gaps even within their embraces. The fog clung to their skin, unexpectedly warm. Thanks to the mist, they were finally able to realize their ultimate passion and joy.

"From now on, I'll go to you once a year," he murmured.

"From now on, I'll go to you once a year," she murmured.

From then on, they'd each go to the city where the other lived once a year; they'd spend the rest of their lives this way, year in and year out. They even conjured up the words "the rest of their lives," and when they pondered these words, they both felt tragic and wretched. Reflecting that "the rest of their lives" could be even longer than the lives they'd already lived, they were, in the end, able to think about it bravely and generously.

At this point, they became a little childish: under cover of darkness and mist, there was no need to feel embarrassment: they could say without shame foolish things out of keeping with their age and experience (people are sometimes very keen on reliving their childhood, even when inappropriate). They asked what he loved about her or she about him, and then said that love needed no excuse. Many times they repeated the sentence that love needed no excuse, in that way finding an excuse for themselves.

The barrier of mist was so dense they couldn't see a soul, and no more than a dim outline of each other's faces. They sat on a cold stone step beside the highway, clasped in a long, imprudent embrace. This mist filled up every tiny space between them, sinuously separating them and then penetrating their whole being. They felt themselves dissolving, dissolving into the mist, their actions and talk also set adrift until they no longer seemed to be themselves.

The next day the sun didn't rise, and the mist turned into a steady drizzle that continued throughout the afternoon. Everyone therefore stayed in for a conference in the hall, a discussion on literary matters. The scintillating speeches seemed to have dried up, and it became rather tedious. Even when two or three argumentative types got going, they weren't able to stir up more than a ripple of interest. The editors and journalists who'd rushed over to the resthouse in spite of the rain gazed anxiously at the writers' mouths, hoping that pearls of wisdom might suddenly pour forth.

Nevertheless, little by little time dragged on. The rain snaked down the windows, making the scenery outside bend and curve in line with the undulating water. The temperature had dropped, and even wearing a wool sweater she felt chilled. She sat by the window, her notebook propped open on her knees, gazing at the dripping scenery outside the dripping window.

Far away, the mountains were almost hidden by the rain, very pale and almost invisible. At this distance, however, the mountains seemed to have come to life, imbued with intelligence, and full of vitality: refraining from talk the better to preserve a secret, refraining from movement in the hope that people would leave, and leave them alone. To come to the mountains for pleasure was in fact to invade them; unwilling to betray their secret, the mountains treated the public with silence. This is how it was. When she turned away, leaving the mountains in the distance, for in the distance, she felt that they began to move behind her back.

He was sitting at the other end of the long table, almost entirely blocked off by the others; only one hand was visible, holding a cigarette between his fingers. He was playing with a cigarette pack between his thumb and ring finger, setting it upright, putting it down, setting it upright again, putting it down again, turning the pack over and over on the table. Looking at his hands, she felt a sudden tremor remembering that it was this pair of hands which had embraced her: these hands. These hands were unfamiliar, and because they were unfamiliar she became more conscious that they were a man's hands. She trembled, filled with an almost ecstatic pleasure; she felt like a virgin in her first contact with the opposite sex.

She was a married woman, and because she was married, she was so accustomed to the male that she'd stopped being conscious of sexual difference and the nature of opposites. She'd spent her life with a member of the male sex; cooped up in one room, they'd soon lost their inhibitions, concealing nothing from each other, keeping nothing secret. They'd lost their sense of sexual difference, and in consequence had also lost the mystical tremor it bestowed. She'd so far forgotten this tremor that it had become a stranger to her, and when it now recurred, it felt like first love: he seemed to be her first man.

However, he wasn't, after all, her first man: she'd experienced this tremor before; it lay buried deep in her memory and her body. From deep down, it now sprang unconsciously back to life, striking an old chord in response to this new summons, so that the present vibration went beyond all previous vibrations. Several strings were plucked simultaneously, so that while she was aware of the strength of the vibration, she couldn't distinguish the different tones within it. Because her long-dormant senses had rested sufficiently, and because she'd been lonely for so long, she'd become ultra-sensitive; the tiniest push was enough to suffuse her whole mind and body with a sensuous joy. Since her marriage she'd slept too long: the mysteries of sex were an open book to her, not requiring from her the slightest imagination or curiosity to explore or investigate. Everything between husband and wife was laid bare: no effort was needed, nor was there any call for shame, although so many sensations which give pleasure are inextricably linked with shame and become insipid without it. Occasionally she would set her lazy mind to work, trying to recall her earliest contacts with her husband, but no matter how she racked her brains, she couldn't remember or even imagine any reason for him to provoke shame in her; this man seemed to have been born beside her, issuing from the same womb. She didn't feel that he was a man and she didn't feel that she was a woman.

But now, as she gazed at his hands holding a cigarette and playing with a cigarette pack, at a distance, almost across the whole room, she discovered men again, and again became conscious that she herself was a woman: she'd regained her sexuality. Oh, how passionately he'd kissed her yesterday! What ecstasy, to be a woman loved by a man!

A wave of excitement surged through her heart. She couldn't sit still, she had to move. She controlled herself, knowing he was watching her: he thrust his hand out between the intervening shoulders to look at her. They could look at each other not only with their eyes but also with their hands, just as they could hold a conversation without words. Nevertheless, she still couldn't help sighing.

She sighed deeply. Happiness filled her heart and had to have an outlet. Immediately aware of having betrayed herself, she turned her head in an attempt to avert attention. The mountains suddenly stopped moving and gradually disappeared into the distance. Although in fact they still occupied their whole territory, they vanished from her sight: her line of vision pushed them away, it went with them; in her dazed state it seemed that even her body went with them.

A new self was slowly being born in the mountains. In this renewed second life, she was supremely conscious that she was a woman—a woman—how fortunate to be a woman, able to love a man and to be loved by a man. It seemed to her that she had only developed a sexual consciousness that day; she was certain that this knowledge was supreme. Even when she forgot everything else she didn't forget this but remembered it at every single moment. It was only because she lacked an opportunity to display it, like a stage on which to perform, that she became profoundly lonely and depressed. She was too conscious that she was a woman; no other woman was more aware of it, or demanded more to know it, or needed renewed evidence of this knowledge more continually, or was more deeply afraid of losing it.

But she realized now she would never lose this awareness: it had died and was now reborn. A woman's self-awareness was advanced and strengthened by a man's attention. Fortunately she'd met him. She was a fortunate woman, she thought with satisfaction. She would demand no more from life, and was filled with compassion and sympathy for all other people.

That night, possibly as the result of a chill, her roommate became sick. Between bouts of vomiting and diarrhea, the young woman writer tossed and turned the whole night, and through it all, she sat up with her, carefully and patiently looking after her, tremendously tender and considerate. Both grateful and apologetic, the girl found it hard to express her emotions in words. For her part, she simply said that she was just doing her duty.

In the back of her mind, she was even vaguely grateful to her, grateful that at this particular time her roommate needed her care and tenderness. Otherwise she would have been gasping for air, on the point of suffocation. She looked after her, but her eyes saw him: he was everywhere, he was always there, he seemed hidden in everything she touched; and she was always tender with him, always loving. Everybody came in turn to see the patient and express their concern. He came too, sitting in an armchair opposite the patient's bed with his hands on his knees and chatting with the girl about very ordinary matters. His composure alarmed her. She even began to wonder if everything that had happened the previous night had only been an illusion—hadn't actually happened at all. If it had all been only in her mind, then. . . . It was too horrible.

Her face was near to betraying her inner turmoil—she could hardly wait for them to finish talking. She needed a chance to verify what had happened the previous night. But there was almost no opportunity. She summoned up her patience and sat down in another armchair beside him. Separated from him by a low table, she joined in their conversation, still feeling uneasy but keeping a grip on herself. As they talked they occasionally exchanged glances, friendly and composed as if nothing had happened, or as if everything was over: it had all been her misunderstanding and imagination. She couldn't help blaming him, but she didn't dare reproach him. She was afraid of making him retreat; she didn't want to make him retreat. She wanted him to go forward.

At this point, he stood up to go. She stood up too and saw him to the door. Her heart was pounding and she was almost trembling as she accompanied him, expecting something but not knowing what to expect. The girl had her eyes fixed on their backs, and there was no way they could evade her gaze. He opened the door, stepped out, and then half-turned to close it behind him. In the final moment before the door closed, his eyes looked deeply into hers. There was nothing ordinary about this look: it was full of secrets that only they knew. A tremendous joy suddenly possessed her. Too happy to know what she was doing, she closed the door on him, actually shutting him out. But his look remained behind, and she took it with her as she slowly returned to her roommate's bedside.

"He's awfully nice, isn't he?" the girl said. She saw that the young woman was very pleased with his visit, more than with any other, and she felt a surge of pride well up in her: she was proud of him, and especially proud that he belonged to her.

"He writes very well, and as a person he's not like the others either," the girl then said. She only replied, "You think so?" or "Yes." Then the girl told her many stories about him, about his family and his work; she seemed to know quite a few things. She listened quietly without interrupting, her heart brimming with undivulged passion.

Eventually the girl grew tired and lay back to read. She also picked up a book and sat up in bed reading. Between every line in the book dwelt his gaze. His look confirmed everything, it proved everything; there was no more need for her to worry. When she'd read enough she closed the book. But as if it had lost its support, his gaze began to drift away—it needed to attach itself to something solid in order to survive. She was obliged to open the book again. The rain and the streams were terribly loud, drumming in her ears. She wished that the night would soon pass; she wished that the next day would soon come. Night separated them; they could only meet during the day.

When the next day dawned, it was their fifth morning in the mountains. There were still five (similar or dissimilar) mornings before it was time to leave. Reaching the middle day was like climbing to the top of a mountain: what lay ahead was all downhill. In unspoken collusion both began to think about the date of their departure. Each day from now on brought it nearer. Up till now, she'd forgotten that the time would come to leave the mountains, to return home; she'd thought that the ten days would never be over, and never suspected that they would be over in the blink of an eye. They'd planned to enjoy their happiness to the full, never imagining that time would run out. Reaching the end before they'd hardly begun, they had been too immersed, too relaxed, too slow.

Having realized this on the fifth day, they actually could have increased their pace and achieved everything in time. However, they didn't proceed with greater haste. In unspoken agreement they preferred to part on a note of regret. It was, ultimately, safer to part on this note: they had in mind the old saying, "the full moon is eclipsed." They knew very well that love required a measure of distance if it were not to disappear.

Therefore they kept to their original fixed rhythms, although their hearts were full of the anguish of separation. This anguish gave substance to their love, it gave them more to savor. They treasured this pain as much as they treasured their love. The next days were in fact the five days which followed the formal raising of the curtain. Before they'd enjoyed to the full the happiness of meeting, the sorrow of parting was added in a bittersweet blend; within these five days, all of life's experiences were concentrated, intermingling almost all of life's flavors.

To simultaneously experience meeting and parting creates an indescribable blend of emotions. It was a flavor they'd never tasted before, and it hoodwinked this extremely clever pair, who mistakenly concluded that this was really love at last—they had encountered the only true love in the world.

In this respect, they felt no regret whatsoever. Their

hearts were full of pride which was actually vanity: no matter what the future held, they had known love; they would be the only man and woman who had really loved.

To the grief and joy of these five days, therefore, was added the glow of their ideals. This glow shed a light over them (and especially over her boring, insipid life), a light that had never shone before. The whole of her previous existence had been a time of waiting for this illumination, waiting to draw near this light.

In these five days, they sensed the passing of every second. Time seemed to pass close to their skin, across their sight, and under their feet. They could hear it pass, humming like a wave of electricity; they could see it and hear it; they touched it without being able to catch it or throw it into reverse. They were both anxious and help-less.

Within these days, they managed to find some time for themselves even during group activities. On one lunch break, they went to the lake and sat down on the stone steps along the bank, dangling their sandaled feet in the water. They hardly even noticed when some children playing games splashed water all over them.

It took them a long while to talk freely. He said something and then she said something, and when she stopped, he went on; and what they said had nothing to do with love. Each felt vaguely dissatisfied with what the other had said and would have liked to turn the conversation in the direction of their feelings for each other, or even emotions in general. But, when it came to their own turn to speak, they continued to circle distantly around that topic.

Tiny fish as slender as needles darted in and out between their toes, cold and slippery, making them shiver. The sun shone over the middle of the lake. Row boats drifting into the ring of golden water would disappear as if they had simply dissolved, and would eventually reappear, sparkling in the brilliant radiance.

They didn't talk about their approaching separation, although the idea of parting wound constantly around them. In fact, the reason they came to the lake was that each wished the other would touch on their separation first, and then they could pass on from this topic into the realm of their feelings for each other. This was a realm that belonged only to them; it was the only contact between them. But they couldn't seem to enter this realm; straying a long distance from its entrance, they ended up saying things that both of them found tedious. Inside, each waited expectantly.

But time was passing. The sun moved west and the lake grew dark. Boats approached the bank, set off again with a fresh batch of tourists, and approached the bank again. They had very little time yet they were still engaged in mundane chatter. Suddenly, both of them began to wonder if anything had really happened. If it hadn't happened, if it were all a misunderstanding, if there'd been nothing, nothing at all, they still could have come to the lake and sat on these steps, talking about literature, art, Lushan, or even Huangshan hundreds of miles away.

It was because nothing had in fact happened between them that they were actually talking about these things! What had happened previously, what had happened only yesterday, grew dim and faint, as if it had happened to others—they were only witnesses, perhaps witnesses only because they happened to be passing by. The fog and the night had concealed everything, making it complicated and confusing. Without daring to admit it, neither had any idea what to do next.

They both felt somehow disappointed, and to overcome their dismay (because each was secretly afraid that the other would detect it), they increased their efforts at conversation. But they felt emotionally exhausted, and wished heartily that they could finish this dialogue and return to the resthouse.

But they couldn't finish, they didn't know how to wrap it up naturally. Once they'd come to doubt the connection between them, once they'd lost confidence in it, they didn't know what kind of tone to take with each other. It was difficult, after all, for them to adopt an ordinary manner since they'd never felt that way: right from the very beginning the connection between them had been anything but ordinary. It was not an ordinary matter for them to have come here, sat down, and spent almost a whole afternoon together—and yet they'd suddenly discovered that it actually *was* very ordinary. It seemed they'd been fooled.

Secretly they were very angry as well as depressed, but they still weren't willing to give up. They decided to launch an attack; they had to test whether what had happened was true or false. Besides, there was so little time left now. The sun was sinking in the west, and they would be leaving the mountains after three more similar or dissimilar sunsets. When they left the mountains they would part: to leave the mountains meant to separate.

Suddenly, he stopped in the middle of what he was saying (it was a speech about form in fiction), turned towards her, and gazing at her with tremendous force, said: "Marry me, please marry me!"

As if struck by lightning, she felt the sky move and the earth spin round; she felt dizzy, and her sight grew dim. When she'd collected herself, she murmured, gazing at him with similar force: "Marry me, please marry me!"

They uttered these words as if reciting poetry. In fact, they'd never given a single thought to marriage: their love had nothing to do with marriage. They uttered these words before realizing their significance: trying to right a wrong, they'd lost their heads. They both felt they'd gone too far, and after a brief sense of release, they fell silent, each a little embarrassed.

Nevertheless, they could stop worrying: everything was proven; there was evidence that they had not been mistaken. What had happened still existed, and would continue to develop. They didn't have to keep talking about trivial, irrelevant things; from now on they could talk about themselves. However, they still didn't know where to start.

The sun had set behind the peaks, the children playing in the water had gone home, and the mist was creeping in from the mountains; only the fish were still darting between their toes.

"We should leave," she said slowly.

"Yes, we should," he answered. Then, "Don't forget me."

"You?" She sent him a tender but ironic glance.

Their conversation from this point flowed as easily and naturally as water. He asked her what she did at eight o'clock every morning, what she did at noon, how she spent her evenings. She answered each question and then asked him why he asked. So he could think about her, he answered, so he would have some foundation for thinking about her!

She was touched, and paused for a moment. Then she asked him when approximately he could send her a manuscript, and when he asked why she should be asking for manuscripts at this moment, she answered that it was in order to invite him to come and correct it—it was an excuse for him to visit!

Their inspiration flowed without a pause, and their conversation was rich with feeling and wit. Their minds were not only full of feeling but also very original. Their creativity made them extremely happy: they were both in top form, the honors falling evenly to both sides. The more they talked, the more pleased they became with each other. Gradually they invented a secret vocabulary of words that only they could understand. These were actually very ordinary words to which they gave a special meaning. For a long time afterwards, these words had a different meaning for them, so that for quite a while they lost their correct grasp on them and got into such muddles that they didn't dare use them freely in their literary work or in their daily life.

The sun had indeed set below the horizon. Mist shrouded them; silhouettes became blurred. Although they clung so tightly, intimately aware of each other's body, they were still in a kind of daze. It was so wonderful to be in this state that they dared not be greedy, in case it would be destroyed and lost, and in unspoken agreement they decided to return.

They stood and made their way up the stairs. His

pants and her skirt were wet from where they'd been sitting. Looking at the wet, muddy smudge on the back of his trousers, she felt very uncomfortable. She tried to avoid looking at it, but the dirty, muddy print stayed before her eyes. Everything else around was indistinct and yet this mark was terribly clear. Reminded of her own skirt, she tried to stay abreast of him so that he wouldn't fall behind and see its wet patch, and she didn't let herself drop back and see the smudge on his trousers. These wet marks seemed to be gnawing covertly at something beautiful. She felt a pang of regret, as if at some imperfection in her own mind.

He, however, had become more intimate in his behavior than ever before, his hand tenderly draped over her shoulder. Leaning against his loving shoulder, she felt very small and weak. What a lovely feeling it was, to lean weakly against a big, strong body. When they walked through the dark shadows of tall trees, he often turned to kiss her, kissing her forehead, her cheek, her neck, her shoulder with a burning passion.

It was only now that they came to a true, profound sense of their separation. Ah, they had simply not dared to let their thoughts dwell on it! They also felt the passage of time, flowing away through the rustling shadows, through the twilight between sunset and moonrise, through his stream of kisses. In her joy and grief she almost burst into tears.

"I don't want you to leave," she was moved to say, grasping his sleeve.

"I don't want you to leave," he said, tightening his arm around her slender shoulders.

Sadly and happily, she thought how nice it was to be

with him! How good it was to be next to him! When she was with him, her entire consciousness revived and became active; her powers of reasoning were also heightened. Both consciously and unconsciously she sifted through her attributes, bringing the good things out for display—she felt as if she were making an offering—and she suppressed those things which were not so nice. She seemed to be engaged in a constant process of improving herself. She felt that she had changed for the better, that from the good things in her she had fashioned a new true self. She considered this self to be a more authentic self. She loved it, she loved it very much, and hoped that she would always be this self.

When she was with him, when they were together, she was confident that she could preserve this self. Therefore, you could say that she loved the self she was when she was with him perhaps more than she loved him. But she wasn't conscious of this now: she was deeply in love with him, and deeply sorrowful at the thought of having to part from him. It was only after many years had passed that she began to understand this.

Grief bound them inextricably closer as the day of their separation pressed inexorably near. Finally, the day came.

It was a morning heavy with mist, as if every scrap of fog had come down from the mountains to see them off. With visibility no more than five yards ahead, the bus set off very slowly. The highway hugged every bend of the mountain, turning this way and that every few paces. They were taking the road down the southern face, stopping at Brocade Peak for lunch. Brocade Peak would be their final stop.

As the bus inched forward through the mist, everyone was sweating with anxiety; they were the only ones who were relaxed. They wished that the bus would go slower, even slower, and that the mist would be even denser, so they could arrive late at Brocade Peak and gain an extra mist-protected evening there. Night would separate them from their parting; night would make their parting that much further away.

At this moment, they were full of yearning and regret, thinking about the previous evening. The days before had been so precious, but they hadn't treasured them, they'd wasted so much.

The bus drove down the mountain, lurching from side to side. All the highway lights were on, but they only succeeded in making the white soughing mist into a vast expanse of whiteness, tightly sealing the road before them from view. Suddenly the feeling arose in them that the way ahead was unknown—a feeling of fatalism. They felt bewildered; they didn't know where the bus was taking them; they were drifting with the wind, bereft of all sense of purpose.

The bus kept sounding its horn, but the horn was muffled by the mist, and the sound, like sobs from another world, didn't carry far. Outside their windows was a world of obscurity, and finding themselves enclosed in this vagueness, they relaxed. They were a little tired, lost in thought, numbed. Their thoughts faltered, they even stopped thinking about their separation. Minds and bodies swaying with the bus, they let it take them to whatever unknown destination.

Slowly, so slowly, level by level, the bus wound its way down. The mist finally thinned out, and they saw the dim yellow lights of another bus loom towards them. The two buses honked as they passed. Afterwards they saw small groups of shadowy figures; they were people walking through the mist. As they passed by, they pressed smiling faces for a moment against the bus windows. The sudden appearance of these grinning faces through the mist was bizarrely unexpected, even a little frightening. They also heard a faint sound of laughter. What were they laughing at? Slowly and laboriously they set their thoughts into motion again.

The mist dispersed. They had reached the plain, and around them fields stretched to the horizon. The bus flew along the dirt road like a song, leaving the mountains glimmering palely behind them.

With the mountains gleaming at their backs, the sky brightened and the sun shone high overhead. Their eardrums suddenly vibrated as the world burst into noise, awakening from sleep. The bus tooted its horn cheerfully, its wheels hummed along the road surface, and everybody was talking at the top of their lungs.

She felt bewildered, and in her daze it occurred to her that all the sounds of the last few days had actually been covered by a thin layer of film. What kind of a joke were the mountains playing! Wilfully playing games with peoples' consciousness! Once this film dissolved, reality was suddenly revealed, its sights and sounds clear and distinct. The world was actually like this—sound was actually like this.

She heard her own voice; she'd actually been chatting

with the others all along, without realizing it. Her voice
had mysteriously changed, oddly strange and familiar,
but she knew it was her own voice, the voice she had
spoken with and heard so many years. She opened her
eyes as if waking from sleep, but drowsiness still lingered;
she felt slightly uncomfortable, her mouth tasted sour,
but she was fully conscious.

It was terribly noisy in the bus, and a popular song on
the driver's radio drowned out everything else: "One
plus one plus one plus one, Put them together means two
plus two, Your heart plus my heart beating as one, Put
them together means I love you!"

She moved in her seat, and fresh energy flowed
through her body. The bus overtook tractors, trucks,
even cars as it sped towards Brocade Peak. They reached
Brocade Peak around noon; their fantasy of spending the
night there had already died and been forgotten. As they
returned to the world of clarity, they felt temporarily
confused, at a loss; they needed guidelines. They seemed
suddenly to have woken from a dream, and for a brief
moment they even forgot each other.

It was wonderfully tranquil at Brocade Peak, and the
water in Dragon Pool was marvelously clear. A stream of
running water flowed in continually from far away, and
drained out again. The pebbles at the bottom were
washed smooth and shiny. Everyone took off their shoes
and socks, rolled up their trousers, and stood in the pool.

The shiny pebbles softly massaged the soles of their
feet. Each grain of sand was clear and distinct, more
distinct than dry sand. The water was even more pris-
tine, more transparent, more unsullied than air. Com-
pared with this water, the air was actually musty. She

stared raptly at her feet in the water, the pebbles under her feet, and the sand around the pebbles. After a while, the others said they wanted to go and see the sights, such as the terrace where Li Jing had studied. She didn't want to leave—she so luxuriated in the water—and stayed behind. He didn't want to leave either, and stayed as well. The others told them not to linger too long, to keep an eye on the time, and make their way to the gate to board the bus in an hour's time. Then they left, shouting and calling out as they moved away.

It was only then that she remembered him and he remembered her. They stood silently facing each other. Finally they waded a few steps towards each other through the water until they were standing together. They both felt awkward, as if they'd become unac-customed to each other.

"If I'd known he was staying too, I would've gone," she thought hypocritically.

"If I'd known she was staying too, I would've gone," he thought, also hypocritically.

By letting their irritation show openly in their expres-sions, they ended up feeling more at ease.

"How pleasant it is here, I wish we could stay longer," he said then.

"How pleasant it is here, I wish we could stay longer," she said too.

This seemed to express their true feelings.

The water was a clear turquoise, without a speck of dirt. They saw the tiny veins on each other's feet, the fine hair on their toes and the cracks in their toenails. They were blocked again, unable to break through the barrier. After having opened the door between them, they had unwittingly closed it again; there was no way through. They'd lost the key and couldn't work out what to do. Too preoccupied even to think about their separation, they stood in the water, numb with misery. After wasting more than twenty minutes in this way, they were both exhausted. They withdrew into themselves, wishing they could abandon this weary, fruitless confrontation.

He was the first to give up. He took a step back, sat down on a stone beside the pool, and reached for a cigarette. At this she also relaxed. She withdrew to the side of the pool, three or four steps away from him. Then he pulled out his lighter, flicked it, and brought it close to the end of the cigarette. In the second when the flame came into contact with the cigarette, something was suddenly illuminated, and both of them gave an involuntary shiver: without exchanging a word, they both recalled Brocade Valley, and its miraculous wind.

He lit the cigarette with a hand that trembled slightly. She slowly sank down on a stone a few steps away from him. They each sat on their stones in silence, gazing at the Dragon Pool spring, which lay deep in the cliff, remote and secluded. Time was passing, second by second. She could even hear the second hand of her watch, "tick-tock, tick-tock," like a bell tolling, and everything before her eyes disappearing into the sound.

She was extremely agitated. She had to know—this was their last moment, everything was about to end— what should they do now! They had actually said and done what needed to be said and done, but she felt what they'd said and done was not reliable, not real; she couldn't fully believe in it; she couldn't fully trust in it. She needed something more actual and substantial, something she could grasp hold of. But she didn't know what this more tangible thing should be, whether it was a word, a vow or a keepsake—all these seemed too frivolous.

She was so upset that she was on the point of tears, but with an effort she contained herself, lowering her head. He also hung his head in dejection. Only ten minutes remained before the bus left, but they couldn't for the life of them think of a way out.

She started to wonder whether she should have taken those three or four steps away from him. At such times, the slightest move can spell disaster: had she already committed a fatal error? If just now she hadn't stepped away from him but towards him, and sat on that small stone beside him . . . but was there still time?

He was already getting his shoes ready. The clear drops of water slid down his heels into the pool, falling without a sound. Then he put on his shoes. They were an ordinary pair of leather sandals, light brown in color, and very worn—there were large cracks in the leather. Then he stood up and was about to move. Where would he go?

Her whole body was tense, and her blood raced. Some naked boys were playing in the pool. She watched them opening their mouths and splashing water high in the air, but she couldn't hear their voices.

He took a step forward. In what direction was he heading? Would this step spell the final disaster—or its opposite? She almost stopped breathing. But he was walking towards her, he was actually coming to her, and when he reached her side, he said:

"Let's go, it's time now, we have to be getting back."

Many days later, when she recalled this moment, these
words became a kind of incantation:

Let's go.

It's time now.

We have to be getting back!

But at this moment, she hadn't time to feel disappointment; she was transfixed with joy. She felt his hand
resting on her head. Every last drop of blood rushed to
the top of her head, every last drop of her blood rushed
to experience and to respond to his hand, every last drop
rushed to kiss his palm. And his palm spread coolness
and warmth, which radiated through her head and into
her blood, causing her blood to flow back, pulsing hot
and cold. Her whole body was shivering, running alter-
nately hot and cold.

She started to put on her shoes, but her feet wouldn't
fit into them until he removed his hand. She stood up,
climbed the stairs after him, and went into the kiosk at
the top. In unspoken agreement they paused there and
turned back to take a last look at Dragon Pool. This was
their last stop. They would never return in this life—
never. If they were to return, it wouldn't be the same
pool, and they wouldn't be the same either. But they
wouldn't understand this until long afterwards. At this
moment, they were only conscious of a profound anxiety, misgivings gnawing at their hearts, but they didn't
know the reason for their apprehensiveness. In fact, every moment and every place in life is unique and can't be
revisited. However, not every moment or place contains
a warning or calls up such anxiety, and so people don't
treasure them—or they only cherish this moment and
not that one.

This they would never comprehend. Despite being extremely clever, they still found it difficult to rise above conventional thinking. And now, as they stood in the kiosk and looked back at Dragon Pool, seized by a hundred different emotions, they were unable to identify them and lapsed into melancholy. Their last minute had passed. He had no choice but to leave. She had no choice but to leave. And as if anxious to push on, they walked hastily away. They had no chance to face each other again: they'd already heard the bus sounding its horn beyond the entrance a long way away.

They really were on their return journey now.

It was already six o'clock in the evening when they arrived back at the provincial capital. There was a letter from her husband, a letter from her office, and a train ticket for the following afternoon. At this point she finally acknowledged that her return journey had begun.

Her husband asked what had happened to her—why there'd been no letter from her since she'd left. The letter from her editorial office was business: they were hoping she could bring back a manuscript from a certain writer, because they were still lacking a lead story for their next issue; the writer had promised them he'd produce one within a few days. She felt a pang of regret that this writer wasn't him—they could have had a reason to see each other again. From now on they would need an excuse to meet; without one it was hopeless.

Down here it was not the same as up there. Life up there had no particular purpose, no center; you could do what you liked. In the world down here, everyone had responsibilities, and people's aims were very clear; you always needed a rational motive or excuse. This was a world of strict causality: all behavior was connected by causal relationships; everything went by the rules. Up there you could go for a walk without any particular destination in mind. Down here, walking always had some purpose; even if the object wasn't very clear, it was still necessary to have one.

It was no longer possible for them to see each other when they felt like it; they had to mingle with the others, watching each other hopelessly from a distance. Often distracted or interrupted, it was impossible for them to even watch each other with a single-hearted devotion; they themselves even contributed to these distractions. They once more assumed their own responsibilities, hemmed in again by a host of miscellaneous tasks which barred them from seeing each other with the eyes of their pure selves. In fact, enmeshed by a profusion of trivia, their very selves were also transformed.

Only three hours had passed, a hundred miles traversed, but suddenly they were very far apart. Yet they wouldn't give up, they wouldn't give up, they wouldn't give up. They would try as hard as they could to hold on—to hold on to each other by whatever strange and curious means.

Those ten days and nights in the mountains had consumed too much of them: their feelings and spirits, their trembling and emotional anxiety. To declare abruptly that all of this was null and void would be too ironic, too cynical, too humiliating. They could never accept this.

It was very difficult to find pretexts to meet and much easier to find excuses not to be together. Indeed, they confirmed their contact by not taking part in the same events. That evening, the organizers of the conference held a final reception. All participants attended, but when he was there, she had to leave; later, when she attended, he left. They were both very quick to understand this wonderful kind of conversation, and were deeply moved by such true love. No longer able to meet, they would be forever parted, but in avoiding each other their souls grew closer. From this meeting without meeting, they derived a bitter pleasure.

The moment of parting finally arrived. He left in the morning, accompanied as before by the writer wearing glasses, but not, this time, by her. Before the car set off, everyone shook hands with them and said good-bye. She shook hands with his companion but not with him. They shook hands passionately by not shaking hands; they gazed fondly by not looking at each other; they exchanged profound farewells by not saying good-bye. Then he got into the car, closed the door, and departed.

She was the first to turn away of those who'd come to see them off. She went into the hotel and entered the elevator. The elevator went up, floor by floor, till it reached hers. She got out and walked along the crimson carpet, proceeding one step after another towards her room at the far end of the corridor.

With the whole length of her back she gazed after his car disappearing into the distance. She would draw near him by running in the opposite direction. The further apart they became, the closer she felt to him. She would try her best, using every means at her disposal, to retain him—to retain the days and her feelings when he was with her. She wouldn't let them slip away, she had to catch them.

But she felt her heart emptying, becoming blank. She heard the elevator door opening behind her, and a crowd of people swarmed out. The corridor was full of confused footsteps, muffled by the carpet. She opened her door, went in, and closed it. She saw her own luggage, packed and ready to go, and she thought that in the afternoon she would also be leaving.

Her train departed at four p.m. The platform gradually receded into the distance. She wanted to fix it in her memory, but there was no special feature to remember it by. It was exactly the same as every other platform; even the attendants who stood there solemnly were drawn with the same brush. She could only gaze back at it as it disappeared from view. The train entered the countryside, heading towards the setting sun.

She was on her way home. She was on her way home. She thought vacantly about home; she couldn't even grasp what home meant. She gazed blankly at the scenery flying past out the window, turning the word "home" over and over in her mind as if trying to extract some meaning from it.

The wheels hitting the railway tracks occasionally produced a resonant clang, like a bell tolling. Her whole mind reverberated with these sounds, leaving no room for her thoughts. As soon as it got dark, she lethargically climbed into the middle bunk, lay down, and went to sleep. She'd forgotten about dinner, and she couldn't even work out what it meant when she heard her stomach rumbling.

The train rumbled and roared, jolting her from side to side, jogging her dreams, scattering them into fragments. In her dream she would try desperately to piece the fragments together, like a child's jigsaw puzzle, but without ever fitting them all in. Nevertheless, the dream continued: sometimes she found herself at Dragon Pool, sometimes in Brocade Valley, and sometimes walking up the nine hundred and fifty-six steps, weary and tense. The steps no sooner appeared in her dream than they collapsed, scattering in all directions. Still desperately, tensely fitting the pieces together, she did her best to understand the dream, trying until her strength was exhausted. But when she collapsed in exhaustion, she suddenly heard herself babbling. In fact she'd been talking the whole time: telling about something, complaining about something, speaking very tensely, very excitedly, very wearily. She was still babbling on and on, unable to stop herself.

She didn't know why she was so enraged. It was terribly unfair, and she wanted desperately to explain this injustice. She was simultaneously indignant and weary. She'd been so noisy the whole night, she was fed up with her own noisiness. Her ears had gone deaf, her voice was hoarse, and her head felt swollen. When she woke up the next morning her head was aching.

The train stopped at a small station. With a sour taste in her mouth, she watched people walk in and out of the station. Some passengers got off to brush their teeth in the platform washroom. White-coated attendants walked past, vacantly pushing food-carts. Across the track, a group of people were fooling about at the ticket booth. A bell rang.

The bell continued to ring insistently. It seemed to arouse a memory in her bewildered mind, but when she tried to clear her thoughts, the memory had gone. As soon as the bell stopped, the train moved forward. The picture of her husband running after the train rose before her eyes. She saw the platform recede faster and faster, but her husband's figure seemed to get closer and closer.

At this moment, she began to understand something. Gradually she recalled the uneasiness she'd experienced when she saw her husband running so strenuously alongside her train. Before the train had started, she'd suddenly wanted to tell her husband something, so she'd started to talk about defrosting the meat in the refrigerator. And again, just before she'd boarded the train, she'd quarrelled with her husband for no reason.

The loudspeaker was announcing that the next stop was the last one for this train. She'd soon be home, yes, she'd soon be home. Her home gradually jutted forward in her mind like a sculpture in high-relief. She felt a shiver of excitement, her heart beat faster, and she had a sense of nervous anticipation.

She didn't know whether she was pleased or not to be going home, nor was she sure if she'd missed home during her twelve days away. She was just filled with a nameless excitement which increased the nearer the train drew to its destination. In the end she was simmering with impatience.

The train entered the urban area. Vehicles and people on their way to work crowded against the level crossing gates. Before the train pulled into the station, a spirited march was played over the loudspeakers, creating the atmosphere of a victorious army returning home. She felt a slight anxiety. Suddenly she regretted not having sent a telegram asking her husband to meet her at the station.

Yes, she should have sent a telegram. There'd been a

post-office counter at the hotel reception desk, but she hadn't stopped there. Thinking about it now, she felt that she had seen it not so much yesterday as in an earlier existence—there would never be another evening dividing yesterday from today so abruptly.

The train finally came to a stop, slowly, gradually. As soon as it stopped, she felt too overcome with lethargy to move. But she had to move. She straightened her dress and tidied her hair, rumpled from being slept on. Her mouth tasted sour; she hadn't brushed her teeth; her saliva was thick and rank. In disgust she tried to block her throat with her tongue to avoid the aftertaste. Finally she pulled her suitcase out from under the bunk, joined the crowd, and moving unconsciously, got off the train.

The sun was high but the wind was quite chilly. Since she'd left, people had started wearing their autumn clothes. Making an effort to keep her spirits up, she walked down the long platform towards the ticket gates. A luggage van suddenly drove past from behind, forcing people to the side. Several tracks away, another train was about to leave: a bell was ringing, and there was a whistle blast. The morning air was fresh, and people wore their morning faces, bright and clean. She was aware of looking pale and untidy but she didn't care. Her only concern lay in mechanically moving forward across the big square. The suitcase dragged heavily at her hand. Not bothering to change hands, she hooked her other underneath for support. Making her way step by step as best she could, she managed to cross the square.

The sun shone down on the busy main avenue in front of the square as if over a river. There was something both silly and magnificent about the scene. She stood, watching the endless stream of heavy traffic, wondering how to cross to the other side. There wasn't even a ferry over the river. Perhaps the zebra-striped crosswalk was a kind of ferry, but the traffic flow was so fast that even the crosswalk wasn't safe. After several unsuccessful attempts, she finally grabbed her chance when the traffic slowed down for a second and dashed across.

She gradually recovered her self-confidence after crossing the street. Her memory of the noisy urban din revived and she soon got used to it again. Striding firmly ahead, she made her way to her bus stop. She wished now she could reach her front door in one step. Her overnight dress and overnight face made her depressed and uncomfortable.

It was half past nine when she got home. Her husband had gone to work, leaving a note on the gas stove. He wrote that she might be home today; there was some frozen mung bean soup in the refrigerator, and some fresh bread; also the thermoses had been filled, so she could wash her hair and take a bath.

The note was dated two days ago. It seemed that he'd been waiting two days for her. There was a sudden tingling sensation in her nose, as if she were a child who'd been punished unjustly coming home.

At this point, her heart was almost overflowing with tenderness, but when she turned away from the gas stove and the note on it, she saw the room was in a complete mess. Dirty teacups lay everywhere: on the chest of drawers, on the bedside cupboard, on the desk, on the table; one was even perched on the narrow bedrail like a bird roosting in a tree. The breeze blew a dustmouse like a ball of cottonwool out from under the bed, and it danced nimbly in the sunlight. The table was covered with leftover soup stains, and the rank smell of floor rags permeated the whole room.

She let out a long breath, fighting back her tears. Resentment rose slowly inside her. She longed for someone to bear the brunt of her anger, but unfortunately for her there was no one else in the room. The whole building was as quiet as if not a single person was there. She could only mutter to herself.

Fuming with anger she started to tidy up the cups, but halfway through she felt like brushing her teeth and opened her suitcase to find her toiletries bag. At the same time she started putting away her clean clothes in a drawer, but something was wrong with the drawer and she couldn't get it open. When she finally managed to tug it free, she saw that the clothes inside were jumbled in complete disorder, spilling out over the sides so that the drawer jammed, and leaving no room for anything more. She set about straightening it up, but as she started to pick up her things she noticed how dirty her hands were—they hadn't been washed since the previous night. Grabbing her toiletries, she hurried out to wash off, but the sink was filthy, so she ran to fetch the cleanser to scrub it. For a while, the more she rushed the more muddled she got, and she ended up getting nothing done.

Tired and angry, hungry and thirsty, she just wanted to lie down, but the bed was piled high and there was no room for her. She was so angry that the tears welled up, her heart pounded, and a vein in her temple began to throb. It really wasn't fair, it really wasn't fair!

She continued tidying up, muttering furiously to herself; her lungs felt like they were about to explode. As if deliberately taunting her, the sunlight grew brighter and brighter, becoming so alluring that it made her uneasy: it made her feel apologetic about whatever she was doing; it made her feel that whatever she did would be unworthy; she ended up not wanting to do anything.

At this moment, somebody shouted up from downstairs. It turned out to be the postman, calling someone on the fifth floor to sign for a registered letter. Her mind grew suddenly agitated. It occurred to her that he might write to her—yes, he was bound to write. Although it wouldn't be today or even tomorrow, it was possible that he might write the following day, or the day after that.

She could wait for his letters: letters wouldn't go astray, letters could record everything; they could be grasped, retained; they could give her a basis for memories and recollections, something which wouldn't be all over in a moment, like a kiss or a few whispers at night in the mist, with only the two of them present, without witnesses.

Thinking of him and of how he might write, she calmed down a little, feeling slightly ashamed that she'd worked herself up into such a rage. She also felt she'd behaved badly, letting herself get so slovenly and irritable. His eyes appeared again before her, and his gaze made her force herself to calm down, to moderate her temper. She'd almost forgotten how tranquil she'd been.

Her mind was in absolute turmoil, but she knew herself that it was wholly unsuitable. It also occurred to her that if she couldn't calm down, then for those ten days she'd hookwinked him, cheated him. Under this severe self-castigation, her rage gradually subsided.

Later, calm and composed, she continued tidying up. As her work became more orderly, the results began to show. When she'd washed her hair and taken a bath, her mood became serene and tranquil. She lay down on the bed, inwardly calculating when his letter might arrive, and imagining what it would say. At this point she was sufficiently at ease to think about him. She considered him in such a clean, neat, clear, and calm sort of way that it couldn't possibly sully him, or the relationship between them. Anything else would have made her uncomfortable. He and she must meet in an environment of almost saintly purity, free of anything trivial: only under such conditions could they converse. Now, it was possible for them to converse.

She smiled tenderly, settled herself comfortably on the bed, and closed her eyes. But her mind was a blank; she didn't know what to think about. Her eyes closed, she concentrated, trying hard to think, but she still couldn't come up with anything. Vague, fragmentary impressions floated by, but she couldn't grasp them; she could only note them as they passed. She might have been telling herself a story, but a story which seemed to have nothing to do with her. She felt tired, and then drowsiness overcame her. Her last conscious thought was that she might meet him in a dream. After that she knew nothing.

When she opened her eyes, the room was hazy and a cold wind blew in through the bamboo blind. She pulled over the blanket and wrapped herself inside. Her body ached lazily as if after a hard day's work, but it was also snug. She heard the pitter-patter of rain and knew it had begun to shower, but no matter how heavily it poured, it couldn't frighten her: she was home!

She now felt that home was an excellent place to be, truly a safe harbor. There was a distant rumble of thunder, and inside the room it was getting darker and darker. But she knew that it wasn't night; there wasn't anything to be afraid of. Raindrops pattered on the balcony. A faint thread of daylight filtered through the bamboo curtain and fell on the mirror of the dressing table, which reflected the dim light. Drowsily, her eyes half-closed, she felt the bed rocking lightly, lulling her to sleep like a cradle. The last image she saw before she closed her eyes completely was a yellow leaf drifting down outside through the bamboo blind: just at that second it flashed brightly, perhaps at the very moment that a dark cloud moved aside in the sky.

When her husband came home and saw his recently absent wife lying peacefully on the bed, he longed to wake her up and talk about everything that had happened during her absence, but he checked himself. He felt that his wife was more adorable when she was asleep than at any other time, and besides, he hadn't seen her sleep so peacefully for a long, long time.

He began to make dinner, moving about on tiptoe. She woke up to the smell of rice burning. When she opened her eyes, she saw her husband clumsily peeling an onion. Touched, she vowed inwardly that she would never lose her temper or nag him again; she would be calm and patient, gentle and tranquil, just as she'd been in the mountains.

The mountains were far away, beyond her reach; she searched for them in her memory but without success: there was only a heavy mist. A pair of eyes gazed at her through the mist. She couldn't disappoint these eyes or they would fail to recognize her, mistake her for someone else. She must protect the image these eyes held.

It was a tender, sentimental evening. A light rain pattered continuously outside the window. The clean, tidy room was illuminated by a milky-white circle of light from the ceiling lamp. It was extraordinarily peaceful and quiet. No one came knocking on the door; it only occasionally creaked with the wind. There was a women's volleyball match on TV, its intensity serving as a foil to the relaxed atmosphere of the room.

They talked in a leisurely fashion about what she'd seen and heard at Lushan, while she pictured to herself the scenes where they'd been together. His appearances were so natural, so unforced, neither too many nor too few, and too unobtrusive to disturb their harmonious mood. From time to time her husband interrupted her with various trivial events which had recently happened at home or at work. The clock on the chest of drawers ticked away. The kettle on the gas stove let out a whistle, and he went out into the kitchen, poured the boiling water into a thermos, and then fetched a mop from the lavatories to wipe the floor where the water had spilled. When he'd finished all this, he came back inside, sat down on the rattan chair beside the bed where she lay, and continued talking to her. The things they discussed

were supremely unimportant, without the slightest significance, not worth recording, but they wove a peaceful
and pleasant evening.

In perfect contentment her husband went to bed and
turned off the light. It never occurred to him that there'd
actually been three people present this evening—not
two but three. For a long time afterwards there would be
three, not two, of them, living peacefully together. There
wouldn't be any strife or conflict: all strife and conflict
would vanish like smoke because of the third person's
unseen presence. Her husband only wondered vaguely
why his wife had suddenly become so calm, but he was
so pleased that she was good-tempered—trusting to luck
that he'd continue to enjoy her good temper—that he
preferred not to bother about anything else.

The next day she went to her office, walking through
the autumn leaves which covered the ground. He seemed
to follow her to work, gazing with unwavering eyes at
her, not missing a single falling leaf slipping past her
forehead. She could feel the attention of his gaze on her
hands, her feet, her forehead, her cheeks, constantly and
everywhere. His gaze seemed to merge with the sunshine
into a single beam to penetrate every nook and cranny.
Even when blocked by a dark cloud, it was transformed
into daylight which spread its rays to clothe her body.
When evening came, the sun entrusted his gaze to the
moon as it entrusted its own light. Whether there were
sunshine or rain, clear skies or clouds, it would never be
too dark for her to see her hand in front of her. As long
as there was one ray of light in the world, there would be
his gaze.

In this way she went to work, joyously treading the autumn leaves which covered the ground. The parasol trees on both sides held hands above her head. Few leaves remained on the trees; their handsome, gnarled bones stood out clearly, and a blue sky glistened beyond the network of interlaced branches. It was like walking down a long gallery whose ceiling and walls were covered with paintings. She gazed around with a fresh sense of new curiosity. On the other side of the road, a young mother was holding a child, who sobbed in a sing-song voice: "I won't go to kindergarten, I won't go to kindergarten," while the mother was trying to talk her round. The sobs lingered on the dappled road behind the mother and child for a long time, like the twittering of a bird.

She saw a four-story building standing in front of her like a big ship. Water stains crept like shadows down its cream walls. The brilliant autumn sunlight rinsed the building and the marks disappeared, leaving it fresh and bright. Its round porthole-like windows glaringly reflected the sunshine, like a row of gleaming mirrors. Inside the green fence was a pot of canna with bright red flowers. She stopped outside for a while and looked through narrowed eyes at the building which she had been going in and out of for ten years, as if seeing it for the first time in her life. Then she said to herself: "I'm here," and walked up the stairs.

On the way to work, she kept speaking to herself the whole time in a low, quiet voice. She could not let him be neglected while he occupied all the space around her; to be worthy of his gaze she had to engage in conversation with him.

It was very quiet in the main building. She was half an hour late, deliberately half an hour late; consciously or not, she was hoping for a small display of welcome—at least she would make people notice that she'd returned. She was back, back from a long way away and a long time ago. She was back at last.

She walked lightly upstairs, her heart pounding, her palms chilly. She felt she was coming back from so far away and so long ago. She wiped off some water stains and gripped the smooth banisters for support, and as she pushed them away under her hand, she felt she was rising above the staircase. She heard footsteps behind a door, but no one emerged; the sound remained inside. Reaching the top of the stairs, she went into the large office.

The office was unusually quiet. The whole staff was there, all working at their desks, completely absorbed and involved in their work. A bird was singing outside. She didn't know how to announce her return. Just opposite the entrance where she was standing she saw the few steps leading to the chief editor's office: back then, it was on those steps that the deputy chief editor had told her—There's going to be a writers' conference, at Lushan, you're to go there! Her heart swung violently, like a boat suddenly losing its rudder in the water, and then steadied itself again.

Restraining her palpitations, she took a few steps forward. Someone finally raised his head: it was Mr. Zhang, but his back was towards her; he'd lifted his head to talk to Mr. Li opposite. It was when Li raised his head that he saw her walking towards them. Li stood up and said: "You're back!" Then Mr. Zhang turned around, and Mr.

Wang, who was sitting by the southern window bathed in dazzling sunlight, also stood up. Everyone turned around, nodding and smiling, saying: "You're back!"

Miss Xie, who sat by the northern window, ran over. "Where've you been?" she asked.

She looked at Xie in surprise, wondering what she meant. Several people all speaking at once informed Xie that she'd just got back from a writers' conference at Lushan. Xie suddenly understood, and said that she'd thought she was on sick leave! It was only then that she remembered that Xie herself had been at home resting after an abortion when she'd left.

Suddenly feeling depressed, she nevertheless forced herself to respond politely as she walked to her own place by the dazzling window. Her desk was quite clean: Wang had given it a wipe every day when he did his own. On the middle of the desk was a pile of manuscripts she'd left unfinished. The one on top had been left open, turned to page twelve. It was written in a dense black carbon-based ink, and the writing was very precise and neat. She touched it and found it was covered by a thin layer of very fine dust.

She heard everybody saying: "How time flies! It seems only yesterday." Then, the interruption over, the room returned to its calm routine, everyone immersed in their own work. Wang continued to talk to her in a low voice, telling her who'd come to visit and who'd telephoned during this period, and how he'd answered their questions or asked what they wanted; he'd noted it all down on her calendar on the corresponding days.

She thanked him and went to look at her desk calendar, at the same time sitting down in her armchair.

(Wang had also kept her chair clean, so she didn't need to worry on that account.) She leafed back through the calendar: Wang had recorded all visits and calls for each day, all very clearly, not missing a single detail. She turned back to the day she'd left, where she'd written in pencil: To Lushan—(she didn't know why she'd used a dash). She held the flimsy pages between her fingers and thought: this is all it was, this and the dust on the manuscript; this is all those days were. Heavy-hearted, she slowly turned back the calendar page by page.

Wang had immersed himself again in his manuscript, a ball-point pen in one hand and a cup of tea in the other. The cup was a glass screw-top jar without a lid, and steam curled up from it. When she'd finished with the calendar, she pulled out the right-hand drawer. She knew that whenever she was away the mail clerk always put her mail in that drawer. As expected, there was a pile of letters inside, which she slowly opened and read one by one.

A fly was crawling on the other side of the window-pane. Its tiny, hairy feet laden with millions of filthy bacteria clung to the smooth glass as if by magic. It made a squeaking sound, like a tiny saw cutting the glass.

Wang softly stood up, went over to the thermoses in the corner and poured hot water into his jar.

Behind the fly was a tall paulownia transplanted from the remote northwest. Beyond its few remaining leaves, the ivy on the wall of the red brick, Western-style cottage in the next courtyard had turned yellow. A small, flowered quilt was hanging to dry over the semi-circular balcony railing. The attic window was open, revealing the upper half of a person. It looked like a girl, wearing a blue pinafore dress. Her head was bent and for a long time she didn't move, as if reading. On the other side of the iron gate a postman was shouting something inaudible. A woman hurried across the courtyard and opened the door. The postman went inside, stopped in the middle of the courtyard and raised his head, still shouting something inaudible. The figure in the attic still didn't move.

When she'd finished reading the letters, her mind was a blank, as if the bottom had dropped out of it and everything had fallen through. She knew she was waiting for his letter, although she knew very well that he wouldn't write so soon. She felt tired and frustrated. Leaning back in her chair, she silently calculated how long it would take him to travel back to where he lived, and how long a letter would take from there to here. This exercise managed to dispel her depression but she couldn't recover her former high spirits. She felt lethargic and bored. Her new burst of vitality that morning had disappeared. Suddenly he was far away and his gaze became indistinct: without his attention and encouragement, she sank into apathy.

The music for the morning break started. Everyone stood up from their desks to walk around, their chairs scraping back on the waxed wooden floor. A few people came over to ask about her trip. Suppressing impatience, she made an effort to rouse herself, and gave an account of the scenery at Lushan.

Her heart contracted with each detail of her story. Every single impression she had of Lushan was connected—blended—with a memory of him. In every description, therefore, she had to detach him from the scene, leaving him abandoned in her mind, wandering alone through the landscape of her mind. Everything reminded her of him. However, without the attention of his gaze, her recollections came to nothing. Like a one-sided love, it left her aggrieved and sorrowful.

The deputy chief editor emerged from his office. When he saw her, he asked her to come to his office after the break to give a report on her trip, and then went out on the balcony and began to jog earnestly up and down in time to the music.

When both morning and afternoon deliveries passed without the letter she expected, she put her hopes on home. Just before parting she'd given him her home address, and he might send the letter there. As the end of the day approached she became excited again. Hope plucked fearfully at her heart, and she felt too restless to sit still. Fortunately, dusk was falling and the office was getting dark, soothing her mood. When the bell rang to stop work, however, she began to dawdle. She seemed to be sure that his letter was waiting for her at home, but just as if he were waiting for her in person, she had to observe the proprieties. At her side his warm gaze gleamed again. Concealed in the deepening twilight, he silently accompanied her.

She felt happy. The tranquil, fragrant twilight air enveloped her, and as she passed alone through the calm redolent dusk, she began to murmur to herself again in response to his warm regard. His gaze passed through her body: she felt its passage; she hoped he would stay within her heart, but he always went away.

She entered the apartment foyer. A sprawling tangle

of bicycles blocked the mail boxes. She pulled them away, opening up a narrow, tortuous path and finally managing to squeeze herself through. She lifted the key and jabbed it agitatedly at the lock. She couldn't help her breath coming faster, as if she were about to keep an appointment, an appointment she'd long been waiting for.

When the box was opened, it contained only the faithful evening newspaper. Her whole body went limp and she almost fell. The path behind her suddenly closed: she was locked in again by the bicycles—there was no way out for her.

She tucked the newspaper under her arm, closed the mailbox, and locked it again. Then with an effort she turned round and made her way out. The bicycles were lying in a tangled heap where she'd pushed them, blocking the entrance to the staircase. She couldn't remember the order in which they'd been stacked before. With her last ounce of energy she shoved them aside to leave a narrow entrance, and then, not caring any more, dragging her feet, she made her way upstairs.

She was obliged to support herself by clutching the rusty handrail, which scraped roughly against her palm. She felt the flakes of rust smoothed under her hand. She went up one flight and entered a pitch-dark corridor. Nothing could be seen; there was not a ray of light. She slowly edged along, relying on her senses and habit to grope her way to her door.

The apartment was in total darkness. She turned on the light, revealing the furniture standing desolately against the walls. Hardly even aware that her eyes were swimming with tears, she was mentally and physically at the end of her rope: all she wanted was to lie down; her only refuge was sleep.

Nevertheless, habit formed over the years now invisibly impelled her forward. Not even sitting first, she put down her bag and the newspaper, and then tied an apron around her waist. This set of movements had developed into a mechanical procedure which she could perform without exercising her brain or making a decision. From opening the mail box to entering the room, she practically hadn't wasted a single minute or hesitated in a single movement, proceeding continuously without pausing for a moment. But in the empty reaches of her mind, she had already fallen many times and struggled up again; she had stumbled and crawled down a long, long road. She was utterly worn out. Her mind was simultaneously bleak and agitated, empty and tense, and finally these confused emotions resolved themselves into anger.

She no longer had to restrain herself, she no longer had to protect her image; she had lost her good temperament, she had lost all her hopes. She started waiting for her husband to return home. If he didn't show up within the next five minutes, he'd be late, and then she'd have a reason to complain. She was hoping he'd give her an excuse to lose her temper, but punctually as usual, his key was trying the lock. He never let her find fault with him: the moment the rice was steaming, the water was boiling dry, and the lid was going on the pot, he'd open the door; she could never find anything to pick on.

But she simply couldn't bear it! He appeared before her and she no longer needed any excuse. Her groundless anger, her bad temper, slipped totally out of control. She was beyond all restraint. She flared up in a towering fury and poured out her rage on him. The meal was cooked and eaten to the accompaniment of her nagging, which continued as everything was cleared away. She went on until she was exhausted and had run out of fresh grievances, then she stopped briefly, still fuming, only to be immediately overwhelmed by resentment and misery. She started to feel sorry for herself and regret that she'd lost control again, and then, with no hope left of ever becoming a new person, she burst into tears.

Her husband, who was accustomed to her nagging and tears alike, found nothing particularly strange in this. After looking on silently for a while, he asked her if she was tired, or if there was anything else the matter. That set her off again, shifting all the blame onto him.

He wanted to go up and comfort her, but she angrily pushed him away. He walked over to read the paper, switching on the TV. The news was on. She shouted at him to turn the volume down—her head was splitting! Before she'd finished rapping this out the noise was gone: her husband had already turned the sound down to nothing, leaving ghostly images moving across the screen.

She was overcome with a sense of tedium. She felt suffocated by all this. The life to which she'd become so thoroughly inured was like a field which had been tilled for so many years that its fresh nutrients and moisture were exhausted—it could no longer produce sturdy seedlings—it lay fallow. Land left fallow might eventually support cultivation again but it couldn't engage one's interest. She was no brave pioneer, either. Wasteland instinctively repelled her; she preferred gardens carpeted with grass and flowers. She could no longer bring herself to reclaim barren ground. She had cultivated her land. With overflowing energy and curiosity, she had cultivated her land intensively, exhausting the soil. Her land had had not four but eight seasons a year. And then she had become disappointed and had let the land lie arid. At present, she kept watch over wasteland, and for this wasteland she wept, grieved, and chafed.

The images on the screen moved silently, and her sobs filled the small room. She could easily have left, gone for some fresh air, improved her mood, but she didn't want to. She insisted on sitting there, watching her husband as if still trying to find fault. She had to make them both feel as uncomfortable as possible, or she couldn't survive the evening.

It was a thoroughly unpleasant evening. After a while she felt a little better. She curled up quietly in a corner of the bed, waiting for her husband to come to comfort her. Her husband would come to her punctually and without fail, to comfort her and to comfort himself. Without such solace, their life would be completely unbearable— or, perhaps, they would both figure out a way to separate. But they always held back at the last second; they never went so far as to risk a real split. At this moment, they would temporarily forget their present disappointment and the disappointment which would come the next day. They learned to forget; to drag out a dreary existence; to live from one day to the next. They kept themselves going like this through countless days and nights.

Her hopes rose with the sun the next day. The fresh morning sunlight brought his gaze. He woke up together with her. She felt that this day would not let her down again. She stretched languidly, thinking languidly.

Every morning she was filled with expectations. Hope nourished her physical and mental energy and restored her body. Everything seemed auspicious to her in the morning. If it was sunny, she thought it was a very good day; if it was cloudy, she thought it was a very different kind of good day! She always left home and came back in excellent spirits, as if she was on her way to an appointment.

But her hopes were always disappointed; not once were they realized. He was gradually and irrevocably leaving her. His image became blurred, his whereabouts uncertain. She could no longer feel his gaze turned upon her, following her. When she tried to recall everything she'd done with him not a single detail was missing, and yet every detail seemed to be something she had invented. They seemed too illusory; they lacked all substance: but at the same time they were too concrete to tally with his overall illusoriness. She found it hard to believe herself that what she remembered could have happened; she started to doubt herself.

She even wished for rumor or scandal, regretting that they had been so discreet at the time. If even a hint had leaked out, it would have been evidence for all that had happened. She longed for proof, but there was none. It was as if he had completely disappeared, had ceased to exist. Where was he! Oh, where was he!

She fretted endlessly. There was no way she could find

him, and without him, she lost all self-control; she simply gave up all attempt at restraint.

But mechanical routine had already formed her daily life. Like a minor planet which had gone into orbit, she could only move within this orbit; she couldn't stop even if she wanted to; she couldn't fall even if she wanted to; she could only advance in spite of herself.

In the morning, she got up and sat on the edge of the bed, drowsy and lethargic, a sour taste in her mouth, a yawn rising in her throat, her eyes blurred with tears. With one leg curled on the bed and the other hanging down so her toes touched the floor, she gave her husband a sidelong look.

He lay there, face up, with his arms and legs sprawled wide. A thin quilt covered him. It was difficult for the sun to come through the flannelette curtain, and the room was dark. The second hand on the clock ticked away.

Then, as if someone had nudged him, he made an abrupt move, retracting his arms and legs. He sat up, holding the quilt around him, his eyelids drooping. He slowly lifted his eyes, looked vacantly around the room, and finally encountered her gaze.

Their eyes blankly traveled across the dark room, and just as blankly crossed. They looked without seeing, like two old houses which had confronted each other from either side of the street for a hundred years. Their investigations had been too impatient: they'd left not a single brick or tile intact; their mutual demolition had been too thorough and too quick: both sides were left in ruins. And since neither had the courage or spirit to rebuild, nor the resolution to walk away, they could only confront each other blankly—or even worse, destroy each other.

Absently he stretched out one hand and groped at the bedside cupboard. The first object his hand fell on was an earpick, and he proceeded to clean his ears. As the pick entered his ear, his eyes narrowed and eventually some expression appeared on his face.

Her mind was remote and empty. Her gaze had already passed through his body, and his gaze had also passed through her: they had permeated each other. They remained as they were, looking through each other, as they continued to do what they were doing.

She gradually calmed down. She'd lost all hope by now. There was nothing in her mind now but a whispering mist, a barrier of mist which covered everything. On this particular morning it seemed that she'd thought through the whole matter. This kind of bleak confrontation was the fate of her marriage, her own fate. She would therefore prefer to bury him behind the barrier of mist—and she would bury his her together with him behind that barrier of mist. She refused to bring him into this desolate wasteland, where they'd be reduced to broken brick and tile rubble, where they'd be razed to the ground. Each cherishing their shining image of each other, they would be buried behind the barrier of mist, deep in the folds of the mountain, deep in Brocade Valley, beautifully mantled by the white cloud. They would return whence they came!

She had set her thinking straight about the whole matter on this morning that was like all the other ordinary mornings. It was now, when she was quite calm and collected, that she realized she hadn't written to him

either. He had also left her an address, she could also
have written to him: they should actually have written at
the same time. There was, after all, some affinity between
them!

Suddenly it occurred to her that nothing, in fact, had
happened. But a string of chance remarks which had
turned out to be prophetic sprang into her mind and
were enlarged: they were—
      All right, all right
      You're about to leave
      I don't want to start a fight
      It's stuffy inside
      Let's go for a walk outside
      First
      Let's go
      It's time now
      We have to be getting back!
      Putting these remarks side by side into one line, she
discovered that they formed a complete sequence: they
formed a complete sequence.
      She felt indeed, in fact, in reality, that nothing had
happened, nothing at all had happened, except that the
parasol tree outside the window had lost all its leaves.
      A story in which there is no story is finished.

My story is finished, but I'm not ready to leave her
yet; I'd still like to follow her. It may not be so simple.
Wearing a light grey autumn dress, she tripped down the
filthy staircase like a girl who hasn't yet left home. The
sunlight seemed transparent: she walked through the
transparent sunlight. She lifted her face and let the wind

blow her hair back. Her mood became cheerful. Behind two locked doors (the one to their room and then the one to the balcony), two sparrows alighted. With their feet together, they hopped this way and that on the balcony and then with a chirp they flew off through the railings.

She saw the withered leaves in the street, rustling between the trees along the pavement. The sunlight transformed them back into gold. They tumbled and rolled in all their glory, brightening the whole street. Almost all the leaves had fallen—the branches were bare. These were the last autumn leaves.

I watch her mischievously pursuing the golden, curled-up leaves with her toe and playfully trample them to make them crackle. It reminds me of what she was like as a child: if something she loved was just a little imperfect, she would destroy it; the more she loved it, the more determined she was. Apart from this, I can't remember anything else. I have to release her, and let her walk away without a story.

First draft September 12, 1986
Second draft September 27, 1986
Shanghai